HER ROYAL REBELLION

ROYALS OF LOCHLAND BOOK III

BRITTNEY MULLINER

HER ROYAL REBELLION

ROYALS OF LOCHLAND BOOK III

This is a work of fiction. Names, characters, organizations, places, events, and incidents are either products of the author's imagination or are used fictitiously.

Copyright © 2020 Brittney Mulliner

All rights reserved.

ISBN-13: 979-8629606390

No part of this book may be reproduced, or stored in a retrieval system, or transmitted in any form or by any means, electronic, mechanical, photocopying, recording, or otherwise, without express written permission of the author.

ALSO BY BRITTNEY MULLINER

ROMANCE:
Utah Fury Hockey
Puck Drop (Reese and Chloe)
Match Penalty (Erik and Madeline)
Line Change (Noah and Colby)
Attaching Zone (Wyatt and Kendall)
Buzzer Beater (Colin and Lucy)
Open Net (Olli and Emma)
Full Strength (Grant and Addison)
Drop Pass (Nikolay and Elena)
Scoring Chance (Derrek and Amelia)
Penalty Kill (Brandon and Sydney)
Power Play (Jason and Taylor)
Center Ice (Jake and Dani)
Snowflakes & Ice Skates (Lance and Jessica)
Game Misconduct (Parker and Vivi)

Royals of Lochland
His Royal Request
His Royal Regret
Her Royal Rebellion

YOUNG ADULT:
Begin Again Series
Begin Again
Live Again

Love Again (Coming Soon)

Charmed Series
Finding My Charming
Finding My Truth (Coming Soon)

Standalones
The Invisibles

To those that believe love never gives up

1

ISLA

I caught Serena checking the time again and fought to keep a smirk off my face. My soon to be sister-in-law wasn't accustomed to how these meetings ran quite yet. She had done it all in the past. Finding the grant or donations, working with the local government for approval, gathering the team of volunteers, and physically aiding in the building of the schools and hospitals. The poor thing hadn't adjusted to how things worked in the palace. I had more resources and a greater reach that I was now offering to her, but it came at a cost. Namely, bureaucracy.

She used to be able to find the need and work at actually fixing it within months. Things took longer here. We had to get approval from what felt like every department of the government. Even as a princess, I had to go through the proper procedures and channels to get approval for my philanthropic efforts.

"We've received permission from the Malawian government to proceed with the plans for the school, but we're waiting to hear back from the treasury on the funds request," said Daniel, the government's head of International Development. He and I had worked closely together for the past seven years.

While I was the royal representative and public head of philanthropy and international aid, he was the one in the background making it all come together. He and Serena would be working closely together as well, but she had to forfeit some of her control if they were ever going to accomplish anything. They were like two wolverines circling each other, silently challenging each other for dominance.

"How long is that going to take? I want to break ground before the holidays." Serena was using her boss lady voice, which I recognized from the times she pushed for what she wanted. She was sweet, kind, and patient most of the time, but she was someone entirely different in these meetings.

"They have two weeks to review," Daniel's voice was tight. He'd told her this nearly every meeting, but Serena didn't like the answer.

"Can't we push it up?"

He leveled her with a look one might receive from an overworked teacher. "No, the treasury must review and approve or reject everything. Not just your projects, miss."

Serena crossed her arms and leaned back in her chair. She glanced at me, and I gave her a sympathetic smile. The same one I gave Daniel a few minutes before. Being caught in the middle wasn't my favorite thing, but I was used to it. I was the peace keeper. The level headed one that brought people together and helped them see the other side of things. Usually with my brothers, but the more responsibility I took on, the more I found myself in this position.

"Thank you, Daniel." I decided it was time to change the subject. "Did you hear back from the suppliers? We want to use local resources and business as much as possible, but I haven't received any responses."

"Only one so far. I've reached out to our contact within

the government to see if they have better luck. If we don't hear back soon, we'll have to make other arrangements."

"Absolutely not." Serena interrupted. "We'll only be using locals. That's the whole point."

Daniel shot me an exasperated look. "We can't build a school without materials and workers. We simply cannot fly down there with our team and hope for the best. We will have to get them from somewhere else."

Serena sighed. "I'll fly down there and talk to them in person. I've had to do it before."

Daniel opened his mouth, but I leaned forward and placed my hand on her arm. "That isn't a practical option anymore."

Her brows furrowed. "Why not? I'm not technically a royal yet."

"No, but you will be very soon. You're no longer a regular woman that can travel alone or go anywhere without being noticed."

"Cian said I would still be allowed to travel."

I nodded, fighting to remain calm even though we'd had this discussion before. "You can, but it requires weeks, if not months, of planning. You can't simply pack a bag and fly to Malawi alone."

She pursed her lips and seemed to resign. I wasn't sure how many more times we'd have to go through this before she accepted it. She knew the cost of accepting my brother's proposal. She was the future queen, but it felt like she was fighting each step along the way.

"We'll keep trying to reach out to them." I shared a pleading look with Daniel, and he agreed. "But in the meantime, we can think about the remodel at Taramore's children's hospital. It's coming up after Independence Day and we still need to decide on a theme."

She lit up at the new subject. "I was thinking we could do

a jungle this time, with lots of animals and some swings and slides in the playroom."

I smiled. "That sounds perfect." I wrote down a few notes and glanced over my shoulder to my assistant, Carolyn. She tapped her watch and I nodded.

"Thanks for all of your work today. Daniel, please keep me updated. Serena, enjoy training."

She groaned. My parents were adamant she went through the same training I had with a special operations team from the army. For two weeks, she'd go through combat training and various attack and kidnapping scenarios. It was grueling and eye-opening. I just hoped she took it seriously and came back with a genuine understanding of what was at stake. Maybe then she'd stop asking to travel to foreign countries alone.

"Now if you'll excuse me. I have another meeting." I stood and straightened my cream, tweed skirt before walking toward the door with Carolyn behind me. I read through a few new emails on my way through the hall to my office. The only sound was the crisp clacking of our heels on the marble.

"Your father has requested to speak to you before your conference call with the Red Cross."

I paused and looked up from my phone. "Why?"

"I'm not sure. I received a message from Ewen during the meeting."

"Do we have time before the call?" It was almost eleven and I hated making people wait for me.

"As long as it's quick. I can start the meeting if needed."

I nodded, grateful she was so on top of things. I never wanted to know what it was like without her. She'd been my assistant for two years, since I graduated from university, but she was also a mentor and trusted advisor. I could rely on her to get things done and I trusted her to represent me whenever needed. That was a rare privilege and I was extremely lucky.

"Thank you. Hopefully I can keep this short." I headed toward my father's office while she continued in the opposite direction. I nodded to the few guards scattered along the first floor. Charlie and Serena found their presence intimidating, but I preferred them being stationed throughout the palace than following me around. It was nice when we didn't have any guests staying in the palace because protocol relaxed a little.

I smiled at the two guards standing on either side of the door to the king's office. "Morning."

Only one of them met my eyes and he gave the tiniest nod. As if a proper greeting would distract him from his job. I knocked once and waited for Ewan, Dad's assistant, to open the door.

Instead, it was Mum that let me in. "What are you doing here?"

Something in my gut told me to be suspicious. It wasn't entirely uncommon for my parents to meet together, but something felt off.

"We wanted to speak to you together." She tried to smile, but it didn't reach her eyes. Whatever was going on, she wasn't pleased.

I ran through the last few days in my mind, trying to think of anything that would have gotten me in trouble, like I had as a child. Nothing stood out. Maybe this was about Cian's wedding. It seemed to be all Mum thought about lately.

I took the soft, oversized leather chair across from my father while she circled his wide desk to face me from his side. They were trying to present a unified front. I knew this well. If it was simply a matter of the wedding or an upcoming event, Mum would have sat next to me.

Dad sat straight with his fingers interlaced and resting in front of him. "Thank you for coming, Isla."

Like I had a choice. The king requested my presence.

I looked between them, waiting for the bomb to drop on my head.

"We've come to a decision and wanted to let you know in advance of the announcement."

Were they getting a divorce? Had someone died? Why were they both so grim? "What is it?"

"We are inviting appropriate suitors to the palace."

I peered at Mum, waiting for her to explain her husband's ludicrous statement. Her eyes dropped to the floor, and I knew this was bad.

"What do you mean? Cian is engaged. You've given your approval. They're getting married in just seven months."

Dad's blank expression didn't waver. He gave nothing away. "The suitors aren't for him."

My stomach plummeted. Oh no.

"They're for you." He confirmed my worst nightmare.

"That's ridiculous. I'm only twenty-three. I have no plans of marrying anytime soon."

"Your mother was married and expecting Cian when she was your age."

I looked up at Mum and her eyes flickered to mine before she turned to face the window. She didn't agree with this, so why was she letting it happen? Dad wasn't some tyrant. He ruled with my mother at his side. They always discussed things and came to an agreement before major decisions like this.

"I don't understand." My hands were shaking so I clasped them together on my lap. "I'm not required to marry, and I mostly certainly will not agree to an arranged marriage."

"You will do as you're told." He growled out the words.

I felt like I'd been slapped. My father never used such a

tone with me, and he hadn't forced something on me since I was a child and wanted to wear pants to events like my brothers.

"Is something else going on? Is there a threat or agreement in the works? What benefit are you after?" I knew this wasn't just about me getting married. It couldn't be. Cian was engaged, Aiden wasn't far behind, so why were they worried about me? The people had plenty to celebrate for the next few years. The news and media had enough to keep them occupied, so why was I being offered up?

"We're not after anything, Isla," Mum finally spoke up. "You know how important it is for us to maintain our relationships with the other families and governments. This is just a step toward that."

"We don't have conflicts with anyone." At least, not that I'd been told. "This isn't the 1500's. We don't establish trade routes through marriage anymore."

"That isn't what this is about," Dad countered.

"Then what is it? Give me the honest answer." I never challenged my parents like this, but I'd never been pushed so far into a corner. I wasn't going to smile and take this silently like I usually did.

"You will do this because it is what I ask of you." He slammed his fist on the desk but I kept my head high and never broke eye contact. He taught me how to negotiate and get what I wanted, now I was going to have to use it against him.

"Will I have to pick one of them? What if I don't love any of them?"

His eyes narrowed. "You will do as I say, Isla. You will choose one of the suitors. Each of them is more than suitable."

"What if I don't?" I kept my voice level, not showing my panic.

"Then I will have to take another look at the budget and see if renovating the children's wings are the best use of our resources."

My jaw nearly hit the floor. "You can't do that." He wouldn't dare punish sick children to control me.

"Don't push me." His clipped tone made my blood run cold, but I wasn't giving up yet.

"How can Cian, the future king, marry whoever he wants. An American, at that, and I have to endure whatever titled idiot comes through the door? Why am I being made to marry a stranger, but my brothers can marry whomever they please?"

"Because you are a princess. You aren't going to take the throne, so you have the option to marry out of Lochland," Mum tried to explain.

"I am not a bargaining chip. I will not be used for the crown's gain!" I sucked in a breath, struggling to keep my composure. "You cannot marry me off to the highest bidder."

I jumped to my feet and hurried out of the room, ignoring my parents' calls. I stormed past the guards and used the back staircase to get to my suite on the third floor. I hoped to see Logan, I could use one of his reassuring smiles right now, but Kyle was on duty. I nodded and he gave me a slight bow I chose to ignore rather than correcting him. He was always so formal and tense around me, and I didn't have the energy to put him at ease at the moment. Just like everyone else, he could survive the rest of the day without me putting on a front. Carolyn could attend my meetings and reschedule everything else. I needed to escape.

2

LOGAN

I rubbed my hands over my black wool pants and tugged at the neck of my emerald jacket. Twenty minutes had passed since my appointed time. Nothing in the Marines ran late. Something was going on.

Each second that passed filled me with more panic. Were they discussing me? I wasn't up for promotion, so this couldn't be a good thing.

"Corporal McCready, the sergeant is ready for you." The petite receptionist pointed toward the hall on her right.

"Thank you." I stood and straightened my uniform before heading toward the office. I knocked on the door and waited for the call to enter.

Sergeant Brown was sitting behind his desk when I walked in. I saluted him before he asked me to sit. "It's good to see you, McCready."

"You as well, sir." His friendliness wasn't unexpected. I'd been reporting to him since I was assigned to the crown two years ago. After my third tour in the Middle East, the opportunity to guard the royal family in Ballivaughn came up. It wasn't as exciting as being on the front lines, and most of the men in my squad looked down on the position, but after my last tour, the passion I'd once had for fighting had dimmed. I knew it was important, but so was guarding the leaders of our country. I took the assignment and was shocked when I was tasked to be the head of Princess Isla's security.

"I apologize for the delay, but I was waiting for confirmation on something before we could talk."

I sat up even straighter.

"An opportunity has presented itself, and you were the first person that came to my mind."

"I appreciate that, sir."

The corner of his mouth twitched up in a hint of a smile. In the two years I'd known him, I'd never actually seen the man grin.

"The position is a special task force that you would lead. I can't give you too many details but it means a promotion and quite a lot of travel."

That would mean leaving the palace. Leaving Isla. The sergeant was looking at me as if he expected me to jump at the chance. It was an offer I would have loved a year ago, but now... I was having a hard time imagining it. A life away from the royal family?

"I appreciate the offer, sir. I'm not sure—"

"You are coming up on your service anniversary." His gruff voice was softer than normal. This felt more like a causal check in than an interview. "You didn't mention wanting to be released last year, but if that's what you want, I can make arrangements."

I shook my head. "I'm not sure that's what I want either."

"I understand. This was unexpected, and you're not required to make a decision today. I want you to take some time and be certain about your decision."

"Thank you, sir."

Sergeant Brown leaned forward, resting on his elbows on

his desk. "Off the record, how have you been?"

"Good. Actually, things have been going very well. I was able to put some new security measures into effect that I'm really proud of. I'm happy to be in a position where I can influence things and make changes. That was one of the hardest things for me before. I was just a cog in the machine. Someone that took orders and executed them. Now I have the ability to think for myself and have my voice heard."

He looked pleased. "That's great. Some go a bit stir crazy in the palaces. They miss the excitement and danger."

I chuckled. "Then they don't go out with the family enough. The paparazzi are terrifying. They will do anything for their shot. I've never met a more fearless and reckless group of people."

His lip twitched. "I really am pleased you are happy there. It's a big responsibility. It takes a special person to endure the lulls and still be on their toes when the moment comes that they're needed."

"I agree. It's a unique challenge."

"Have you thought about what you want to do after this?"

I tilted my head. "What do you mean, sir?"

"Do you want to make this your career? Do you want to eventually return to civilian life? Do you have any passions you want to follow?"

I scratched my jaw. I'd been wondering the same things for a while. I kept putting off making any sort of decision for a while, simply letting my contact renew each year in hopes something would help me make up my mind. "I'm not sure."

His eyebrows raised just a hair. "What was your plan when you first joined the Marines?"

"It was all I wanted growing up. I wanted to serve our country. I never loved school. I didn't want to go to university and end up in a cubicle for the rest of my life. I wanted to be out in the world."

"It's been seven years now." He pointed out.

"It has. I still feel like this is what I'm supposed to be doing, but I've been a Marine my entire adult life. I haven't had time to figure out what else I'm passionate about."

He nodded. "I'd like for you to think about that while you consider the special task force position. How much longer do you want to serve? What is your plan? What do you want your future to look like? We'll touch base soon."

"Thank you, sir."

He excused me and I left his office feeling less dread but much more confusion. His questions were simple. I should've had answers for them, but I didn't. He was right. I needed to think them over and make some important decisions.

When I got back to the palace, I checked in at the security office. It was a large room under the east wing that housed the surveillance footage, armory, and could also be used as a bunker in case of emergencies. It was bombproof and at least three guards were stationed there at all times.

"All clear?" I asked Bill, the head officer down there, as I took the open seat next to him.

"Nothing to report." He tipped his head in the direct of a screen that showed the front gates. There were three media vans parked, but otherwise it was empty. "It's nice not having any guests or events for a bit."

I didn't argue with him. Things had been mad with the wedding, then with Prince Cian and Prince Aiden bringing home girlfriends. We had at least one paparazzo a day try to break into the palace. Thanks to the security system I developed, we were alerted immediately and they were removed. Since the news of their relationships became less enticing, things had calmed down. You wouldn't hear any of us complain about that.

Her Royal Rebellion | 13

"I'm going to check in with Shane. Let me know if anything comes up."

"Of course."

I left the palace and crossed the grounds to the guard bunker. It was a two-story building made to look like a barn, but inside was a kitchen, living room, ten bedrooms with two bunk beds each. After living with my squad in the desert for months, it felt like a luxury hotel to only share with three others. Plus, usually only two of us were sleeping in there at a time with our shift rotations.

Shane and I were the leads on Princess Isla's guard. There was only an hour a day that we both had off, and we used that time to coordinate any of the princess's events.

I walked into our room and found him sitting on his top bunk with a book on his lap. He glanced up and grinned. "How was your meeting?"

I began pulling off my formal uniform. The king preferred the guards inside the palace to wear suits so we could blend in better. Only the men that worked along the perimeter and outside the gates wore the emerald and black.

"It was interesting."

He set the book to the side and dropped to the ground. "How so?"

"Sergeant Brown gave me a few options I wasn't expecting."

His eyebrows rose. "Like what?"

I hesitated. "I'm still processing. I'm not ready to talk about it yet."

He gave me an easy smile. "I understand, mate."

I knew he would. He'd been in this world long enough to know there were no easy decisions. "I've honestly never thought beyond this. Joining the Marines was my only goal."

His face dropped. "You never thought about anything else?"

"You have?"

"Course." He chuckled. "Thinking about my options is what keeps me going half the time. I can go back home and help run the family pub until my dad's ready to retire and then I'll take it over, or I can move to the city and work security somewhere. I could even travel for a while."

I fell onto my bed. "See, I've never considered anything like that. I don't have a family business to take over. Mum's a teacher, and Dad's retired from the army."

"You could always stay. Make this your career."

I nodded. "I guess that's what I've always defaulted too. Sergeant Brown wants me to really think about my plans and figure out what I want next."

"Good for you. At the end of next summer, I'm out. I knew eight years was my limit, and I'm past that. It's time to get my payout and finally start my life."

I never felt like I was waiting to start my life while I'd been in the service. This was my life, but was it all I wanted? I wasn't sure.

"You'll figure it out, mate. Don't worry." He headed out for the second portion of his shift, and I leaned back against my pillow. I should rest before I needed to take my post, but my mind was racing.

If I wanted to stay in the service, taking the special task team would be the right move. It would come with a promotion and further my career. But I loved my job here. I was good at what I did, and I'd earned the princess's trust. That had taken time and a lot of hard work. I didn't want to give that up. Staying here would be the hardest choice. I knew my feelings for my charge were wrong, and pointless, and would end up hurting me. If I was a smart man, I'd leave now. Any day I'd be forced to watch Isla fall in love with someone else. That would kill me. I wasn't worthy of her. No one could ever be, but as her guard, I stood no chance.

I was responsible for protecting her. Her wellbeing was my number one priority, so I should want the very best for her. I should want her to be happy with some duke or billionaire that could take care of her. I was a commoner. No one. I was delusional to think that anything would ever change between us.

If she ever found out how I felt, she would stop trusting me. She would, rightly, report me and have me moved. I'd lose my position here. I might even be discharged. I could be stripped of everything I've worked so hard for. It would be worth it if she felt the same for me, but that wasn't possible.

The only way I could stay here was if I repressed everything. Pushed down my feelings and focused on doing my job to the very best of my abilities. Maybe, if things got to be too hard down the road I could ask to be switched to one of the other royals. We'd need to build a team for Charlie and Serena soon. It would be a good idea if I volunteered to head one of those, but only if I could accept watching Isla from afar, knowing I could never have her.

That thought scared me almost as much as leaving here and putting her safety in someone else's hands.

The smart thing would be to leave. I should take the new position.

No, that would be running from the problem. I needed to figure out what I wanted out of life. I couldn't make the right decision without any regrets until I had the answers to Sergeant Brown's questions.

I checked my phone to see a message from Isla, asking how my meeting went. I couldn't fight the smile that curled my lips. She had a million things going on in her life, but somehow managed to remember the little things I told her.

I told her it went well and would discuss it more with her later. Unfortunately, I had to wait until my shift to see her.

3

ISLA

I turned the corner and sighed, relieved to finally be alone. Shane was now positioned across from my doors. He nodded when I approached but remained silent. He wasn't the person I was hoping to see. I knew it was inappropriate, but I wanted to see Logan. I needed to tell him how ridiculous my parents were. I shouldn't, but I had a favorite. I looked forward to seeing Logan more than any of the other guards. He was the only one that I felt like a normal person around. He treated me like a friend and that meant more to me than he'd ever know.

Luckily Charlie was the only one who knew how I felt. She was annoyingly perceptive and had picked up on the way I lingered every time I saw him. Could anyone blame me? He was tall, dark, and so very handsome. His muscles could barely be contained by his suit and his jaw would have inspired the great sculptures of old. It was more than that though. He didn't treat me like a delicate flower or just an object to protect.

"Miss." He opened the door, and I stepped into my sitting room. The door shut, leaving me alone with my frantic thoughts. I walked to the windows overlooking the walled garden and sat on the bench, resting my head against the cool glass.

Shane was great at his job, and friendlier than most but he always kept his distance. It took months for him to stop addressing me as Her Royal Highness every time he saw me. He backed down to Princess Isla, which I nixed. Ma'am followed, and it took every fiber of my being to refrain from using my combat training to take him down. We settled on Miss, which wasn't my favorite. I'd prefer Isla, but he refused saying his mother would have his head if she knew. Heaven forbid he call me by my name like a normal person.

Logan really saw me. He was the only guard who bothered talking to me. It wasn't a rule that the guards and security had to ignore us, but most did. Maybe they thought it would keep them out of trouble, but it was dehumanizing. I loathed it. When I was younger and tried to engage them in conversation, I would get one-word responses before being dismissed entirely. I knew they were trained to show respect, but they could at least say hello or crack a smile when I did.

Logan was the best listener. He let me go off on tangents only giving sage advice or feedback if I asked.

And the way he smiled at me. Just the thought made my heart race.

Maybe it was a childish fantasy, but I hoped that one day after he retired from service, there was a chance for us. That he would come back to the palace and sweep me off my feet. He'd declare his feelings, and I'd tell him how I'd always felt for him, and we'd start our own lives. Sure, I would still have responsibilities here, but I could take a step back. We could move to my house on the coast.

I leaned back and shook my head. I couldn't let myself think that way. Logan would never see me that way. He referred to me as a friend, one he was fortunate to have.

A few minutes later, a knock sounded on the door and Carolyn let herself in. Her eyes found mine and a frown appeared. "Is everything alright? You missed the call."

I tried to gather the strength to sit up straight, but I couldn't find enough reason to care. "No, it's not. I'm sorry I should have let you know I wasn't coming."

She moved across the room and sat next to me. "It's not a problem. I was able to get the information we needed and set the date for the meeting in Berlin."

I nodded and looked back out the window.

"Isla? What happened?" Her voice held so much concern, it nearly broke me.

"My parents are bringing in suitors for me. They're making me marry one of them."

She let out a tiny gasp. It wasn't proper for her to question the actions or decisions of the king and queen, but her slip made me feel better. I wasn't the only one thinking this was all mad.

"Why?"

I turned back to her. "That's the worst part. They didn't really give me a solid answer. It was like they were hiding something."

She didn't react this time. Her eyes dropped as she picked off nonexistent lint from her skirt. "I'm not sure what to say. It doesn't seem fair, but he's your king."

"First, he's my dad," I huffed, and she gave me a disappointed look. "Fine. I know that's not the case, but I wish it was. Why can Cian marry whomever he wants? Serena's the future queen, and they didn't care that she's not Lochish or titled. Why does it matter for me?"

She reached out and took my hand in hers. "I'm not sure, Isla. I wish I had an answer or solution for you, but the only thing I know for sure is how much your parents love and adore you. I have to believe that they're doing what they think is best for you."

"I'm not a child. They need to accept that they taught me well and trust me. I don't want to be forced to marry someone I don't love."

She nodded. "You might find someone you like very much. You could grow to love one of the suitors."

Sure, that was a possibility, but it seemed unlikely. Mum and Dad didn't even have an arranged marriage. They'd known each other practically their whole lives. They got to meet and fall in love naturally. Why wouldn't they extend me the same privilege?

"I just don't understand why. Dad went off about my duty, and since I'm so far down the line, I can marry and leave Lochland. Are they trying to get rid of me?"

"Of course not. They love you. I'm sure they just want you to be happy." Her reassurance did nothing for me.

"It's not like I'm an old maid! Cian and Aiden haven't married, so why do I need to?" I rubbed at my collarbone as my throat tightened.

She was quiet before a tiny smile appeared. "You can always play along and simply dismiss each man that comes. As long as your parents see that you're making an effort they might not push things."

"But what if they do? What if I send them all away and Dad demands I marry the next one that arrives?"

Oh no. I was spiraling into a real panic. I wanted to run, but where? How? I was a princess, so it wasn't like I could check into a hotel unnoticed. Not without a team to help pull it off.

"Isla, why don't I take the rest of your meetings for the day? Anything that requires your presence, I'll reschedule."

"Thank you." My shoulders dropped. "I can't think straight right now."

She stood and placed her ever-present leather folder on her hip. "Of course. I'll take care of everything. We do have some decisions that need to be made for the Independence Day celebration but we can work on that tomorrow."

I couldn't believe that had already slipped my mind. It was my biggest event of the year. Mum passed along the responsibility after I graduated, and I took it seriously. I preferred to be as involved as possible with the plans, but I wasn't in the right head space at the moment.

"Would you have my meals sent here? I can't stand the thought of seeing my parents right now."

"Of course." She dipped her head before leaving. The moment I was alone, I fell back against the window and stared out at the gray sky. How could this day turn so quickly? I could daydream all I wanted about running away, but I knew I never would. Carolyn was right, my king had made a decision. It was my duty to follow. I might not understand or agree, but that didn't matter. With all the freedom and privilege I'd been blessed with, there was always that hanging over my head. I couldn't change who I was, who my family was, or the responsibilities that came with it. The majority of the time, I was fine playing the role of agreeable, perfect princess. It was rare for me to want to rebel. I felt childish locking myself in my room, ignoring my role and meetings, but this was serious. It was life altering. I would allow myself one day to ignore the world, and tomorrow I'd put on a brave face and play the part of a dutiful princess.

I moved to my library off the sitting room and found my favorite, worn copy of *Pride and Prejudice* before curling up on the cream crushed velvet chaise in the center of the room.

Mr. Darcy just arrived at Netherfield Park when there was another knock at the door. I debated ignoring whoever it was. Mum and Dad likely noticed I was hiding by now, and

I knew the person would continue knocking until I let them in.

"Come in." I set the book down and watched the main door swing open. Aiden and Charlie walked in and crossed the room toward me.

"Where have you been?" Aiden asked while eyeing the area. He noticed my book and glared. "You've been reading? I wasn't aware you were taking the day off."

His condescending tone did little for my mood. "Carolyn is handling things today."

Charlie urged Aiden to sit down next to her, and she studied me before speaking. "You weren't at lunch or dinner. Are you feeling okay?"

I shook my head. "No, I'm not."

Aiden's forehead wrinkled. "Has the physician been by to check on you?"

"No, Aiden. I'm not that kind of ill."

His eyes widened, and he brushed his hands on his pants. "I can have the kitchen bring up some chocolate cake or that mint ice cream you like. I think they keep it on hand now with Charlie and Serena around."

Charlie looked like she was fighting not to say something, but she just patted his arm. "Isla, why don't you tell us what's going on."

I thought about teasing Aiden for a moment, but it wasn't really the right time. "Did Dad tell you what he and Mum met with me about this morning?"

"No, neither of them mentioned anything."

Of course not. They probably thought I was on board. "They're bringing in suitors for me."

His brows shot up. "What? Why?"

I shrugged a shoulder still feeling defeated. "Dad went on about duty, but it doesn't make any sense. It's like they want to marry me off for some sort of trade."

Charlie gasped. "I thought you guys could marry anyone."

"Me too," I grumbled.

Aiden was rubbing his jaw with a far off look. Charlie turned to him. "Do you know anything about this? Why they would do this now?"

He shook his head. "No, I'm trying to think if there are any deals we're stuck on or anything Dad has mentioned. Cian might know something, but nothing stands out to me."

"We can't let this happen." She sounded as indignant as I felt. "You should have just as much freedom to choose who you marry as Aiden and Cian."

At least one person was on my side. "I don't know what I'm going to do. Dad said he was making the announcement today, so men will start arriving soon. I have no interest in meeting any of them, but Father threatened that if I don't marry one of them then he'll cut the funding for the remodeling project."

"I don't... Isla..." Aiden seemed a bit shell shocked as he tried to speak. "This isn't okay. The children's hospitals aren't up for negotiation. Plus, arranged marriages haven't been done in at least a hundred years. I don't understand why they'd do this to you." He jumped to his feet. "I'll speak to them immediately." He marched to the door and slammed it behind him.

"I can't believe this, Isla." Charlie soothed. "I promise we'll do everything we can to stop this."

I appreciated her thought, but there wasn't much we could do when the king gave an order.

"What about..." Her voice trailed off and she glanced back to the door. "Have you spoken to him?"

I swallowed and shook my head knowing she was referring to Logan.

"It's going to be okay, Isla. We won't let anything happen that you don't want."

She wasn't really in a position to make that kind of promise but it still helped knowing I had people on my side.

"I'm going to see what I can find out. I'll see if I can reach Serena and have her keep her ears open for anything."

She stood and gave me a hug before leaving. Knowing I had my siblings on my side made me feel a little bit better. I'd worried that Aiden would tell me I needed to listen to our father and that he knew best. I should have given him more credit. He knew better than anyone the importance of standing up to our parents and fighting for what we wanted. He never would have been happy taking on his crown responsibilities if he didn't also pursue his dream of LochEnergy. He changed the economy for the country and developed new energy technology that we'd shared with the world. I couldn't picture the man he would be now if he didn't fight to take that path. Hopefully, Cian would be just as supportive.

4

LOGAN

I met Shane in the hall across from Isla's doors. "Everything okay?"

He nodded. "Aiden and Charlie stopped by earlier." It wasn't proper for us to refer to them so casually, but since we were alone, we didn't worry about titles or codenames. We only used those when traveling or in more public settings. "The prince left in a hurry. He seemed rather upset. Charlie left a few minutes later and seemed resigned. I'm not sure what's going on, but Isla hasn't left the room since this morning."

"Has Carolyn been by?" It sounded like something was wrong, but I didn't want to jump to conclusions. I needed more information.

"Yes, just before lunch."

"And did she seem off?"

He nodded. "Yes, there's definitely something going on."

I fought the urge to burst into Isla's room and ask her for myself. That wasn't an option with Shane still here. I'd have to wait and use more discretion.

One of the kitchen staff turned the corner carrying a

large tray. She paused a few meters from us. "Evening." She smiled and looked at the door.

I stepped forward and took the tray from her. "Thank you, I will take this to the princess."

She looked relieved and turned.

"Ma'am?" I wished I knew her name but with over one hundred and fifty staff members on the palace grounds it was a bit hard to remember everyone unless I interacted with them regularly.

She paused and faced me. "Yes, sir?"

"Have you heard anything today?" The housekeeping staff was usually the most up to date on the gossip, but everything made its way to the kitchen eventually.

She looked around as if someone might be watching before stepping closer to me. "Princess Isla retreated to her suite this morning following a meeting with the king and queen. We don't know anything for certain, but we've been told to prepare for regular guests for the foreseeable future."

I narrowed my eyes. "What kind of guests? How many?"

She shook her head. "We're guessing other royals, from some of the requests. We were told to plan on a minimum of ten new guests each week until the king says so."

That didn't make any sense. There were no events coming up. Independence Day was a celebration that brought in the Lochish elite, but it was held in the capital. They wouldn't be coming here.

"Thank you."

She nodded and hurried back the way she came. I turned to Shane. "Does that make any sense to you?"

"No, I haven't heard any of that."

That's what I was expecting. "We need more information so we can plan accordingly. Would you mind working on that? I'll stay here."

He nodded and walked down the hall. I waited until he was gone before knocking once on the door.

"Come in." Isla's voice sounded sad. Tired.

I ignored the sudden surge of my heart rate and opened the door. Isla sat in her study. Her face lit up for a flash before she reined it in. I loved the times when it was just the two of us. When she could be herself without worrying about propriety or an audience.

She didn't move to stand so I crossed the room and set the tray on the table in front of her. "I heard you haven't been attending meals."

She twisted and dropped her feet to the floor. "I haven't been in the right mood."

"Should I leave?"

Her eyes met mine, and I could see the pain. "Please don't."

I sat on the chair across from her and watched as she peeked under the silver dome covering her plate. She sat back and left the food untouched.

"What's going on?" I couldn't control the worry in my voice. I hated seeing her hurting. I wanted to fix it. Fight whatever demons were weighing on her.

She let out a slow sigh. "It's bad, Logan."

Everything about her was breaking my heart. The way she stared at me. The way she said my name. I wanted to reach out for her, to pull her into my arms and make promises I had no way of keeping.

"Tell me."

She held my gaze and I watched as her eyes grew watery. "My parents are bringing in suitors for me. They're trying to marry me off to a stranger."

There was nothing that could have prepared me for that announcement. Now the king's request to prepare for guests made sense, but that was the only thing my brain could comprehend.

"Why?"

She bit her lip and shook her head.

"They're arranging your marriage?"

She slumped and covered her face. I watched her shoulders shake once and it was enough to break me. Before I could think, I jumped up and hurried around the table between us. I sat and pulled her into my arms. I'd only held her like this once before, when she learned about the death of a beloved aunt.

She didn't hesitate before curling into me and crying against my chest, each gasp and sob stabbing me in the heart.

Forget my role, forget decorum. I would gladly lose my job and be dismissed from service if it meant I could comfort her. There was nothing more important to me at this moment than being there for her.

I ran my hand over her hair and tried to whisper reassurances, but I didn't even believe them. How could I tell her everything would be okay when I was pretty sure this was the end of everything?

I longed to tell her how I felt. I would take her away from here. We could be happy together.

That was insane. She was one of the most famous women in the world. She wouldn't be able to cross the street without getting recognized.

"I'm so sorry, Isla." I rested my chin on the top of her head. I wasn't used to feeling helpless, but there was no amount of tactical training that could prepare me for this.

I wouldn't let her be forced into anything. I would eliminate any man that tried to hurt her. I'd protect her the only way I could. There had to be a way to change the king's mind.

After a few more minutes she leaned back and stared up

at me with red-rimmed eyes. "I don't want to do this, Logan. I don't want any of them."

My heart tightened at what her words could mean. Did she already know what she wanted?

"Say the word, and I'll get you out of here. I'll take you anywhere you want."

She sagged into me. "There's nowhere I can run that I won't be found, and I can't run forever. I don't want to give up my life and work here." She sniffed. "I shouldn't have to. I don't know why my parents are doing this. Why are Cian and Aiden allowed to be with the women of their choice? Why can't I have the same freedom?"

I ran my hand up and down her arm. We'd had stolen moments like this before. It was always enough to make me think that just maybe she had feelings for me, too. But then things would return to normal and I'd spend the following days wondering if I'd imagined it all.

"Isla, how can I make this better?"

She met my eyes and I saw longing that matched my own. If only she would say it. Tell me to take the chance. One word from her and I'd give it all up.

"I don't know, Logan. I don't know what to do. I'm scared." She blinked away more tears. "I'm terrified, actually. I can't marry a man I don't love."

I didn't want that for her either. I could live with knowing she met the man of her dreams and they ended up together, as long as I knew she was happy. That was enough for me. But I couldn't stand by and watch her be forced into a marriage. I wouldn't let it happen.

"I'll do everything I can to make sure that doesn't occur." That was the only promise I could make. If someone was disingenuous or made her uncomfortable, I'd find something on them to get them removed. I'd plant information if needed. I might not be able to stand up to the king on her behalf, but I could work on things from behind the scenes.

"Logan." She said my name like a prayer. I studied her face, fixating on her lips for far too long. I'd dreamed of kissing her for a year now, and she was so close. With what her father had planned, this might be the last chance I ever got.

I couldn't do it. Not while she was so upset. I wouldn't cross that line unless I knew she wanted me to. I couldn't take advantage of her emotions.

"Isla, I promise. I will do everything in my power to protect you. Always."

Her gaze dropped and she nodded before tightening her arms around me. We held each other for several minutes. Silently memorizing everything about this moment.

"I should get back to my station." I didn't want to move, but I knew it would raise questions the longer I was in here. Someone was bound to notice. Nothing happened in the palace without someone seeing.

She nodded and leaned away from me. "Thank you, Logan."

I straightened and smiled at her, trying to remain strong for her.

"What about your meeting? What did your sergeant say?"

That discussion felt a lifetime ago, though it was only that morning. "He was just checking in. Nothing important."

My decision was made for now. I would stay here for as long as Isla needed me. I couldn't even consider the possibility of leaving her right now. I had to be here to make sure she had someone on her side.

I stood and walked out without looking back. I couldn't. I knew if I saw her broken expression, I'd stay. That wasn't what was best for either of us. I resumed my position in front of her door as thoughts poured into my head. What if I told her how I felt? What if she felt the same? We could go to her parents and tell them. We could put an end to this madness before it even began. Sure, I was just a Marine, but Serena was the future queen of the country and she wasn't even Lochish. If they approved of her, they would eventually feel the same about me. I knew the king and queen. They liked me. They would adjust to the idea.

That would mean I would have to end my active service. I couldn't continue as her guard, or accept the special task force if we were to marry. I'd give up the only life I ever knew. The only dream I'd ever had, for her.

This was insanity. We were friends and had private moments when we opened up to each other, but she really didn't know me. She didn't know about my childhood or very much about my family.

Did that matter? Was all of that necessary to know how you felt about someone?

Not to me.

We would have time to worry about that. We would have our whole lives to share every detail.

I rubbed my hand over my face. If the king and queen wanted potential suitors to come there must be a reason. We had to figure that out first. I needed to know what I was up against. Hopefully, Shane could find out more about that before I was relieved from my post.

I wanted to get a hold of the list of expected guests as soon as possible. We had the ability to run background searches, we'd be required to since they would be guests at the palace, so I could gather as much information on each 'suitor' before they arrived. Knowledge was power, and in this situation, we needed every advantage possible. I wanted to figure out what was in it for each man that arrived. I wanted to know their weaknesses, their goals, what motivated them and get them away from Isla as soon as possible.

She might have to go through with this act to appease her parents, but she wouldn't be doing it alone. I'd make sure she was armed with the ammunition she needed to clear out these men. If she could give the appearance that she was willingly going along, and the men simply didn't measure up, that could buy us time.

I was going to save her from this. It was my responsibility to keep her protected. That meant I had to protect her heart as well, and I took my job very seriously.

5

ISLA

"Are you sure you want to attend? I can make an excuse."

I appreciated Carolyn's offer, but I couldn't put off my duties forever. At some point I was going to have to leave my room and return to the real world despite how badly I wanted to hide. My eyes kept flicking to the paper peeking out of her folder. This morning, she'd showed me the official announcement sent to the other monarchy countries from the King's office. It said I was entertaining suitors and looked forward to making new acquaintances.

It was all lies. They even had a picture of me and my parents from an event a few weeks ago, the three of us smiling and waving like we were welcoming the world to our front door. It made it seem like I was on board, like I was a hopeless fool that needed my parents to arrange for strangers to come and meet me. It sounded more innocent than me looking for a husband. Almost like I was in search of some new friends. Males only of course.

It was bizarre and I almost asked Carolyn to release a statement on my behalf letting the world know I wasn't a desperate little girl who needed her parents to do things for her. I knew that wouldn't go over well with my parents. Dad would say I was unwell. Soon I'd end up locked away in some long-forgotten castle.

That actually didn't sound too terrible at this point.

"No, I need to attend the meeting with Charlie and the representatives from Sudan. I can't miss that."

"Of course. I've scheduled your lunch with Charlie as well. I figured you might still want some space."

Bless this woman. "Thank you."

She smiled. "The car will be waiting at noon to take you to Robby's pub."

I threw my arms up and hugged her. She wasn't a fan of physical affection, but tolerated me... most of the time. She chuckled and patted my hand resting on her shoulder. "You're the best."

"This afternoon, you have a meeting with Lewis about the next hospital renovation. A light day."

I nodded. I was grateful for that. I wasn't sure how long I could keep a smile on my face today. "I thought you had the meeting yesterday."

"That was for the hospital in Ballivaughn. This is picking out the next hospital. Cian wants to continue to check off each children's wing, even while he's away. So, you and Lewis will be picking the next one."

"We have a list, why don't we just go in order?"

She opened her folder and looked through her notes. "Cian requested we go in order of need."

"Fine. Has Serena chosen her next project?"

Carolyn turned a few pages. "She wants to help rebuild communities from the fires in Australia."

I wrote that down and nodded. "Add me wherever I can help. I'm sure they need schools and hospitals immediately. Maybe we can hold off on the children's wings here for a year. We've updated the most necessary ones, and Australia needs our help more right now."

"I'll send a message to Lewis and you can discuss it this afternoon."

"Thank you." I looked through the rest of the schedule for today and wondered if I'd have time to see Logan since Shane was on duty. I wanted to apologize for losing it on him yesterday. He'd been so kind and gentle. He was exactly what I needed to feel better, but I felt bad dumping my problems on him. Although, he did handle it quite well. The moment he stood and walked away, I shattered. I cried harder than I had the entire day. I realized that was the kind of man I needed. Someone who simply held me when I needed him to. Someone who was willing to stand up for me. That wanted to fix the problems, but knew that sometimes all that could be done was being there for someone.

I would be lying if I said my little crush didn't get a whole lot bigger after last night. I could think in hypotheticals, but really, I knew I wanted all of what he showed me about a good man from *him,* not just anyone.

I had to push those thoughts away. It would only lead to more heartbreak for me.

We gathered our things, but before Carolyn could walk away, I stopped her. "Have you heard anything about why Dad's doing this? Anyone have ideas?"

She shook her head. "Not yet. I'm keeping an ear out for any tips though."

"It would be so much easier to go along with this if they were just honest with me. If there is a plan at play, I need to know what it is."

She gave me a sympathetic smile. "We will figure it out, Isla. I promise."

I nodded and followed her out of my office and down the hall to the garden drawing room. It was Charlie's favorite, and since she didn't have an official office, she liked to work from there.

The queen was happy to share her preferred space as well. Mum used her office more often now to give Charlie space, but soon Charlie would need her own room. Well, that was assuming Aiden and Charlie lived here after they married. They were waiting until after Cian and Serena's wedding since they didn't want to take any of the attention off the couple. I had a feeling Charlie wanted to marry quietly while the rest of the world was still fixated on the future king and queen.

It wouldn't surprise me at this point if they slipped away and eloped somewhere. Our parents would probably kill them, but at that point what could they do? The thought made me smile. At least one of us should get what we wanted.

The door was cracked open, so I pushed it and stepped inside. Charlie was sitting on the velvet settee with papers scattered around her on the circular cushions. She glanced up with a weak smile.

"Good morning."

I sat across from her and took in her tired face. "Morning. How are you?"

She sighed. "I've been better."

I narrowed my eyes. "What's going on?"

"I think it's just stress. I've been feeling a little under the weather, and I woke up this morning with a bad headache."

"Oh no. Why don't you go lie down?" I was growing worried.

"I can't. We've got this meeting and you know how important it is. Plus, I've been getting a feeling lately that I'm being watched more closely." She sounded so exhausted, not just physically but mentally.

"What do you mean?"

"I just always feel eyes on me, and there have been more meetings added to my schedule. I asked Aiden's assistant about it but he had no idea how things were showing up on my calendar, either. He isn't putting them there and it's the most trivial things. Like double checking a guest list or approving silverware for a meal. It feels like someone is trying to keep me occupied." She sighed. "It's been going on for a few weeks, then with what you told me yesterday... I can't help but wonder if Aiden's next. Will they bring in women for him to meet? Try to see if there's someone out there better for him? We're not engaged yet, so it wouldn't be that hard to get rid of me."

Anger ripped through me. My parents were hurting so many of us. I wanted nothing more than to bust into Dad's office and let him know how his announcement was being received by those closest to him, but deep down I knew it wouldn't matter. Nothing could change that man's mind when it was set. The best thing we could do was play along until we knew how to get out of this.

"I'm so sorry, Charlie. I don't think they're trying to replace you. Aiden would never let that happen. He'd leave the crown before letting you go."

She blinked up at me and nodded. "I don't want it to come to that. I don't want to be what breaks up the family."

"It wouldn't be you. My parents are pushing all of us, and it can't go on much longer without one of us snapping. Once Cian catches on, he'll be the first to put a stop to it."

I longed to reach out to my brother, but I knew he was pretty much off the grid. Only Lewis could contact him and it was for emergencies. He took Serena's safety seriously, and training with his old army troop was the best way to keep her safe. They would be back in two weeks, so we just had to wait until then.

"You're right. I just need to stay strong." This world was

new to her and though she handled each change in her life with grace, things had to get overwhelming occasionally. She went from an unencumbered college graduate to a public figure within days. "We have a few minutes before the call. Do you want to review anything?"

I looked over my notes. "I think the most important thing is to convey that we want to get them to a point where they can take over as soon as possible, people trained, provide the tools they need so they can build the windmills, and run them independently. From our first call, I gathered that that was very important to them. They don't want to build an industry that invites people in for the jobs. They want to help their people."

"I agree. The whole point of expanding LochEnergy is to get countries self-sustained. We want to create more jobs and resources for them."

I nodded, and a moment later Carolyn entered and started the call. I let Charlie take the lead, only jumping in when she threw me a look or when the representatives asked me questions directly. I was proud of how comfortable she'd become with leading these conversations. She was passionate about the projects and working with other countries, so it came naturally for her to take over this aspect from Aiden. They were becoming a powerful couple, outside of the influence of the crown, and I couldn't be any prouder.

After the call ended, we left for lunch. Carolyn stayed behind to catch up on other work, so it was just me, Charlie, and half a dozen guards. I looked around for Logan, but didn't see him. They rotated their schedules so often I couldn't keep track. I think that was the point, not letting anyone get too complacent and not creating patterns for an outsider to catch on to.

We walked through the back door of Robby's and

through the dark hall. The pub was less crowded than I expected for lunch time, but it was a nice reprieve.

"There are my favorite girls," Robby called to us as we sat in the booth closest to his station at the bar.

"Hi Robby," I greeted before slipping off my coat and sitting down. I scanned the room and easily picked out the guards, some in uniform and some not. I smiled at the few patrons and fought the urge to apologize. The locals were used to us popping into town to shop or eat on occasion, so it was just the tourists we had to worry about. I vaguely recognized most of the faces, and I figured the guards had already checked out everyone here.

"What are you in the mood for?" I asked Charlie since she didn't even bother pulling out a menu.

"Fish and chips."

I smiled. "Of course."

Aiden got her hooked on that when they first met, and since then it was the only thing she ordered. Robby had some of the best, but it was still fun to tease her.

"I've tried other things. That's just my favorite."

I laughed and Robby came over with waters and two baskets of his famous dish.

"Thank you, Robby. Did you know we were coming?"

He smiled. "Of course. Carolyn called this morning and they came about an hour ago." He nodded in the direction of a table of casually dressed guards. He was used to us by now. Dad came here when he was younger and introduced us to the pub at an early age.

It was comforting to eat here. A slice of normalcy we rarely got. When we came to Robby's, we were just regulars. Robby knew our orders and teased us like he did with all his repeat customers. After the days we'd had recently, it was just what Charlie and I needed. Charlie ignored our conversation while digging into her food. It looked like she was benefitting as much as I was from this outing. Her shoulders relaxed for the first time all day, and she actually paused to smile at Robby.

"Let me know if you need anything else."

I nodded before he walked back to the bar. "Feel better?"

Charlie's eyes twinkled and she smiled. "A bit."

"Good." It filled my heart to see her in higher spirits. I just wished it would last for both of us.

6

LOGAN

"This seems like a waste of time. We're not going to find anything on these guys. Their own countries have the power to bury anything they don't want us to know," Shane pointed out. We were tasked with running background checks on the potential suitors that had already accepted King Leo's invitation to come meet Isla. We were halfway done and so far, every man was squeaky clean. I knew without a doubt that their security teams made sure we found nothing negative and covered any red flags that would prevent us from letting them into the palace.

It had me more than a little worried. This wasn't what we were used to doing. Preparing a venue for a royal event or clearing out a city of thousands of people was easy. Going up against a group as powerful and strategic as our own team made me uncomfortable.

Each man on the list had an ulterior motive. I felt it in my bones. Even Peter, a Duke from Denmark. He and Isla grew up together and were close friends. He was the son of a duchess who was best friends with Queen Anne's cousin. The three women had attended boarding school together, and I knew deep down the Queen hoped Isla and Peter would end up together. I shouldn't let that get to me, and I'd even liked him the few times we'd met, but that didn't mean he was right for Isla. I had a feeling he was coming to the palace at the insistence of his mother and the Queen. I didn't think he was any more interested in Isla than she was in him. Hopefully, he would be another resource for me and Shane. He could spend time with the other suitors and uncover their true intentions.

"I agree. I'm also trying to figure out what King Leo would gain through Isla's marriage to one of these men." I hadn't told him about my conversation with Isla, so it had shocked me when Shane told me he had his own suspicions. I was relieved I didn't have to convince him something more was going on. It could be considered treason for us to talk this way, but our priority was Isla and keeping her safe. We took that seriously, even if it meant questioning her father.

"I know what's in it for Bhutan. Their main ally is India. They're looking for additional support." He tapped on his print out of Lord Ugyn, a close advisor to the Dragon King. "He has a reputation of being incredibly kind, like the rest of their country, but I already know he's coming with a motive."

I nodded. "At least we know. Maybe an agreement can be made without a marriage though. We can advise Isla to hear him out and encourage a discussion with one of her brothers or the king directly."

"Yeah, let Cian deal with him." Shane was as enthusiastic about this as I was, but for very different reasons. He found this suitor business to be a waste of time and resources. He knew Isla almost as well as me, and he knew she wouldn't be forced to do something as serious as marrying someone unless it was her idea.

"I don't know what the king would want from Bhutan, so it's unlikely that match will be encouraged." I agreed with him and he put a red check on the profile before flipping the page.

"Henri Lennoy, Count of Luxembourg. I can't figure out his motive for wanting an arranged marriage." I searched his name and frowned when his picture appeared. He was handsome, wealthy, titled, and a playboy. Every result was a tabloid story about his escapades. The most recent was from the past weekend. How was Isla supposed to believe he was a serious suitor and future husband when he was out partying up until the day he came to meet her?

"Oh boy."

I let out a half chuckle. "He's a gem. He's one that makes me suspicious of his intentions. He doesn't seem like he would be interested in getting to know Isla, unless he's just after a title."

"We'll keep an eye on him." Shane wrote a note on his profile. "Have you heard about any business with Luxembourg lately?"

"No, I'll be sure to mention it to Isla so she can ask Cian and Aiden to look into it."

He blew out a breath. "I feel like I'm back on active duty doing recon and gathering intel from our informants."

"If you like it maybe you should pursue a career in the capital. I'm sure they'd love an agent like you in the intelligence agency."

He barked out a laugh. "No way am I leaving the uniform for a suit and a cubical."

I pointed to him and looked around. "We're not far off at the moment."

He tugged at his tucked in shirt. "This is different. We're still in the middle of the activity. When we go out with Isla, we're the only thing between her and danger. There's still action. They try to make intelligence agents look exciting in movies, but they spend ninety-nine percent of their lives chained to a desk. I couldn't live like that."

The conversation had turned in a direction I wasn't expecting. We never really talked about life beyond this, but it intrigued me to know that he was thinking about what he would do after retiring. We were supposed to be doing background checks, but this was the perfect moment to ask.

"So, what are you going to do? Obviously not a desk job." I laughed to lighten the mood. I didn't want him to realize how important his answer was to me.

He pulled his hand away from the mouse. "I always planned on staying for eight years. I knew the payout would be worth it, and I'd leave at a good station. I was comfortable with that timeline."

"It's been nine years for you now."

He scoffed. "I'm aware. Sergeant Brown pointed that out at my last review. I never expected to be in this position though. I thought I'd be working on the front lines that whole time. When I was offered a position at the palace, it felt like it was a soft retirement. It would be too easy after fighting on the front lines. I only accepted it after Sergeant Brown spent a few weeks convincing me. I didn't expect to love the job."

My chest tightened. Did he have a love for something specific? Or someone?

"Even though a lot of it is routine and standing in the same place for hours at a time, I know what I'm doing is important. I know that Isla trusts us. I know her family trusts us. Is there anything more valuable than that?"

I shook my head. It was reassuring to know he loved this job as much as I did, even without having feelings for Isla. "I agree. I never imagined myself here. When I found out about the position, I knew I wanted to serve the crown. I didn't expect to be this direct. I thought maybe I'd be on the grounds somewhere, but you're right. They trust us and that's huge."

"So, you want to stay?"

"I have no idea."

Should I tell him? I considered him a friend, and he was one of the few people in my life who understood exactly what I was going through. I just didn't want it to get out that I had other options. I didn't want word to spread that I might be leaving, especially before I made a decision.

"Can I ask you something, in confidence?"

He turned to face me, his mouth barely a frown. "Of course."

"Sergeant Brown gave me a few options last time we met. I'm not sure what I want to do."

"Okay, start with the options," he stated calmly.

I appreciated he was treating this logically and not making it seem like a big deal. "I can retire. I didn't put in my year notice, but he said he can work it out. I can stay here. Or he offered me the lead on a special task force. He couldn't give me much information about it, just that it would include a promotion and a lot of travel."

His eyebrows rose. "Interesting." He seemed to be thinking it over. "And you still have no idea what you're going to do?"

I sighed. "No, I honestly never thought about life beyond the Marines. It's been my sole focus since I was a kid. I knew I wanted to serve and signed up the day I turned eighteen. It's been six years and I'm still not sure what comes after this. I guess I never considered the possibility of something else."

He didn't respond immediately, and once again I was grateful he was taking this seriously, not giving me a blow-off response.

"No one can tell you what to do. Remember that. The

most important thing is to be true to yourself. Any decision you make is the one *you* have to live with, no one else."

I agreed.

"I don't think you can make the right decision until you figure out what you want. You really need to consider your goals and what you want out of life. I can be your sounding board and we can bounce ideas and pros and cons off of each other, but ultimately, you won't be confident in your choice without knowing yourself a bit better."

I let out a sigh. "You're right. I have to really think about what I want. Sergeant Brown said I had some time to decide, but I don't want to drag it out. I need to figure this out."

He nodded. "Well, what do you want in life?"

"In general?"

"Sure. When you're eighty and looking back, what do you want to have accomplished? Do you want to be married? Do you want children?"

"Yes. I want a family eventually."

"Okay. That's a huge factor. The next step would be deciding the timeline on that. Is that ten years away? Five? One? If a family is an immediate priority, then I wouldn't recommend accepting the task force. You have no idea how long the mission will be and they're known to be all consuming. It doesn't sound very conducive to a home life, so you should take that into consideration."

That was a great point. Dating would be impossible. Having a wife and children while running that team wouldn't be fair to anyone. I had no idea how dangerous it was either. I couldn't put a family through that.

But was I ready for that life? I couldn't picture myself married either. At least, not yet.

"If that's all a ways off, then you need to think about how long you want to stay in active service. What do you want to do once you're out?"

"I have no idea. That's what I've never been able to envision."

"Maybe you're meant for a military career."

"That's what my father's done. I don't think that's what I want either."

He laughed. "You have some serious thinking to do, mate."

I nodded. "I know. Thanks for letting me talk it out."

"Yeah, let me know when you have some ideas."

"I will." We both faced the screen and continued our task of running checks. The Marquess from Belgium didn't stand out. Then again, a fourth of the country was noble so it wasn't much of a surprise he wanted his chance to meet the princess. It was shocking there weren't more Belgians on the list. Maybe they were taking their turn.

"He won't last a day," Shane said with a chuckle. He wrote down the marquis's interest in equestrian activities. "Isla finds that incredibly boring."

I smirked. "Only those closest to her know that."

"So, he'll be thoroughly disappointed."

"When his thoroughbred horses don't impress?"

He laughed at my lame joke and we moved on to the Count from the Netherlands. Jean was an interesting man but seemed a bit too old for Isla. He was nearly forty and came with his own wealth and successful technology company.

"A title chaser," Shane said with a scowl. "He only dates countesses or above, and they're usually ten years his junior, at least."

I was glad I wasn't the only one thinking that. "I wonder if he's interested in setting up a trade or agreement with the King. He's one we should watch."

Shane added a note then moved on. "Oh no. Please, no."

I groaned when he pulled up the next man. The Spanish

Duke of Carona had been to the palace before, and he was one of the most demanding guests we'd ever had. Nothing in the palace pleased him. He complained about the thread count of the sheets, the temperature of his food, the number of steps to his room. Everything was an inconvenience. I couldn't imagine the queen agreeing to let him visit again.

I narrowed my eyes. "Red flag him. I thought he was banned after the window incident."

He broke one of the original stained glass windows from his bathroom because he was upset it didn't open. It had devastated the queen, and she'd asked him to leave immediately.

"I don't know how he slipped through the cracks."

"I'll have Marianne double check." The queen's assistant was a no-nonsense woman who helped run the palace like a machine. I had a feeling once she found out about Francisco, he would receive a letter kindly uninviting him.

"Just two more left." Shane flipped the page and paused. "Can't we skip him?"

I looked at Peter the Danish Duke and sighed. "Yeah, we know him well enough."

"Good, then it's just..." He turned to the next page. "Lord Marius of Suruso."

I narrowed my eyes and read over the short profile. The small country south of Romania on the Black Sea usually stayed out of the affairs of the rest of Europe's royalty. This would be the first time any of their nobility visited Lochland.

"I've never heard of him," I thought aloud.

"Neither have I." Shane opened a few of the results. "I don't see any red flags though."

I read the most recent article. He was a close friend of his Prince and the heir to a winery that was valued at tens of millions of euros. He wasn't the richest man on the list by a long shot, but he seemed like one of the most normal compared to his counterparts. I immediately disliked him. He posed a genuine threat. He was handsome, wealthy, and seemingly stable. Someone Isla could fall for.

"We need to keep an eye on him." I stared at his picture while Shane wrote a few notes.

"I agree. It's strange their country would be making an effort now. After all this time? What's the real motive? I feel like there has to be something else."

I shook my head. "That's what I don't like."

We finished checking within the intelligence system and broad internet searches before I took his notes to copy and give to Marianne. I wanted her to review them again before any of the guests began arriving. In the meantime, Shane and I had work to do.

7

ISLA

"Surely this is a joke." I eyed the man getting out of a limo and sighed. Henri, Count of Luxembourg, nearly stumbled up the steps. One of the guards reached out, catching his elbow and keeping him upright. "Is he drunk?"

The sight was appalling. I tried to fight my parents on him, but Dad refused to deny his request to come. At least Mum got the Spanish Duke off the list. No one in the palace wanted that man back here, so Dad let that one slide. He was adamant I meet and entertain every man who requested a visit.

Carolyn scoffed under her breath. She wasn't a fan of the Count either. He was like so many other nobles I'd met, wealthy, privileged, and lacking responsibility. I wanted nothing to do with him. He got through life on his name. He'd attended one of the most prestigious universities in Europe, and failed out. He preferred clubbing to finding a way to use his influence to help others.

He might have a pretty face, but that meant nothing when the head was empty.

"How long is he staying?"

"Three days," she replied.

"If he makes it that long. He'll be bored by morning." I dreaded the thought of letting him loose on the town. Heaven only knew how he would terrorize the locals.

There was a knock at the door and it pushed open. "They're ready to announce you." Logan's frown showed how unexcited he was about this.

I tried to convey how upsetting this was with a look and his tiny nod told me he understood.

I knew it was extra work for him, Shane, and the rest of the security team. There was a ridiculous amount of coordination that needed to happen with each suitor's team and then there was the additional risk of having foreign nobles at the palace.

"Thank you." I checked my reflection and smiled at the very modest long sleeve dress that hit below my knees. It was a thick cream tweed that barely skimmed over my curves. I intentionally picked out the blandest, least flattering outfit to dissuade Henri's interest. Once he saw how opposite we were, he'd be running. He wanted flashy and glamourous. I wanted stable and motivating. I wanted a man who would stand at my side and support my philanthropic endeavors. Dear Henri did not fit that role.

"Come along." Carolyn walked in front of me down the hall and signaled for me to be announced.

"Her Royal Highness, Princess of Lochland."

I descended the stairs, locked eyes with the Count, and forced a small smile.

His eyes ran over me, and I cheered inside when his grin dropped a bit. He wasn't pleased with what he saw? Well then, he could turn around and fly home.

He met me at the bottom of the steps and held out his

hand. When I reached him, I placed my palm on his and he raised it, placing a light kiss on my knuckles.

"It's an honor, Your Highness."

Now, my upbringing taught me to treat him with respect and put on the proper performance, but I was also a princess and he was a lower ranking noble. I didn't even need to make eye contact if we were being strict.

Unfortunately, the palace was full of eyes and mouths that loved to rat me out to my parents, so I at least had to play nice.

"A pleasure, Henri." I knew a man like him loved his title, but I refused to use it. I would not play into his ego. "I don't believe we've had the opportunity to meet. What brings you to Lochland now?"

I was still standing a step above him, quite enjoying him having to look up at me. I was very curious about his motives. Shane and Logan gave me a copy of their profiles and notes on each man that was coming, and they were just as confused as to why he was here. He loved partying and made weekly appearances in international tabloids.

I was the complete opposite. The last time I was in a magazine was for my cousin's wedding. I knew that was inevitable given the public's obsession with what the Royal families wore to large events, but I didn't give an interview or answer any of their questions. I wanted my part as small as possible.

Henri seemed to live for the attention, something he would gain quite a lot more of if he were in a relationship with me.

I narrowed my eyes. Was that all he was here for? A photo opportunity? Something to be able to brag about when he returned home?

"Isla, I've been longing to meet you for a while now. The opportunity never arose."

"Princess."

His brows pulled together. "Pardon?"

"You may call me Princess Isla or Your Highness."

He cleared his throat and nodded once. "Of course. Yes, Princess Isla. I'm so very honored to have the chance to meet you now. Perhaps you can show me around your beloved Ballivaughn. I've heard you and your family prefer to live in the town where you can walk the streets and avoid the crowds of the capital."

I nearly burst out laughing. He just arrived and wanted a tour of the town? Not the palace or even the grounds? No, he immediately wanted to go in public. If Carolyn wasn't around to thumb me, I would have brushed off my shoulders at how quickly I figured him out.

He was only interested in the press. Silly boy.

"Actually, I was hoping to show you the lake shore. It's very private." I batted my lashes for added effect but his smile wavered.

"Oh right. Certainly."

I stepped around him and headed through the back hallway. Aiden and Charlie stepped out of his office.

"Isla, where are you headed?" Aiden's steps faltered when he noticed Henri following me. "Oh Henri. I wasn't aware you'd arrived."

They met us and Henri looked a bit flushed. Was he nervous?

"Prince Aiden. You're here."

I looked between them, not understanding the underlying tension. Charlie looked just as curious.

"I don't know why you're so surprised. This is my home."

Henri took a small step back. "I should leave."

Aiden sneered. "No need to leave on my behalf. I'm willing to let bygones be bygones. Afterall, I'm a forgiving person."

I narrowed my eyes at my brother. "What happened between you two?"

"We had a run-in in London last year. Didn't we, Henri?"

I glanced over my shoulder to the man looking around like he was searching for the nearest escape route.

"What happened?" I asked him. His eyes flashed to mine for a moment before studying the carpet with fascination.

"It was just a misunderstanding," he mumbled and Aiden's eyebrows rose.

"A fifteen thousand Euro misunderstanding." Aiden clenched his jaw. "Why don't you explain yourself, Henri."

Charlie looked between the men before smirking at me. She was enjoying this as much as I was.

"Well?" I prodded.

Henri sighed. "I heard Aiden was at a club with some of his university mates and I went down to say hello."

Aiden laughed, but didn't say anything.

"I was there with a few friends, but I couldn't find Aiden. I ordered some drinks while I searched. Then there was a scuffle with some bloke and me and my friends were asked to leave before we could close our tab."

I watched Aiden's expression change from amused to furious in a flash. "Is that really the delusion you're telling yourself?" He watched Henri for a moment. "No, tell my sister the truth."

Henri glanced up at me as his face paled. "Fine. When I got to the club, I let them know who I was and told them I was with Aiden and his lot. Me and my mates drank and then got into a tiff with some locals. We were kicked out and Aiden got the bill for our drinks."

"And the damage you did," Aiden added.

Henri nodded.

"And it wasn't just you and a few friends. It was close to twenty people. You didn't make it past the VIP section. I didn't even know you were there until a server arrived with my bill."

"I've apologized." Henri sounded like a petulant child.

"Yet, I've never received the reimbursement you promise."

"I... I..." Henri stuttered.

"I've got a deal for you." Henri lifted his head enough to meet Aiden's eyes. "I'll forgive your debt and forget about that night if you leave."

Henri froze. He blinked and looked at me.

"Now," Aiden barked. "And you will tell the king and queen that the moment you met the princess you knew you were not worthy."

Henri didn't even pause to think about it. "Of course."

He turned and walked back toward the entry without a single look back at us. I nearly applauded. I caught Logan covering his mouth, but I could see in his eyes he was laughing. Check one off the list. If they all went this poorly this quickly, I might be back to normal life within a week.

"Thank you, Aiden." I hugged my brother, feeling an enormous weight lift from me.

He squeezed my shoulder before stepping back. "I knew having something on him would come in handy eventually."

I giggled. "Yes, it worked out quite nicely. I appreciate you using it for me."

"Anytime." He reached for Charlie's hand and they continued down the hall. I could hear her whispering to him and soon they were both laughing.

Carolyn fell into step next to me and opened her folder. "Well, now that we have the day opened up. What would you like to do?"

I let out a breath. I had a whole day to myself now that I wasn't playing hostess. "Have we received the auditions from the bands for the Independence Day parade?"

She turned on her tablet and tapped a few times until a list of files faced me. "I have them here."

We walked into my office, and I immediately relaxed into my cream chair and took the tablet. She sat next to me and we watched the videos. The first was a drum corps then a pipe band and a few wind bands.

I decided to include three, one of each type, in the Royal parade.

"Now, you must decide on your guest."

I repressed a groan. It was tradition for the princess to host the parade and have one honored guest. If I really had a choice, I would invite a child, maybe one fighting a battle with disease or a winner of a science contest. Someone that inspired me. The guest was usually the most famous pop singer or actor of the moment. It was a crowd favorite and brought an international star to Lochland, a rare occurrence.

Mum had the responsibility for a few years before Dad's coronation, and she told me stories about the celebrities that came. They were fond memories for her. Since Dad didn't have a sister, his mum filled that role almost her entire life. She lived for the event each year. Even as the queen, she loved spending the day with someone famous.

It was ridiculous.

"You can invite anyone you want, Isla. You don't have to follow tradition."

I rolled my head and met her eyes. "You know as well as I do there will be riots."

She smirked but it disappeared as quickly as it had appeared. "Fine. Are there any actors you have a crush on? A singer you would like to perform?"

I thought of Logan immediately. He was the only one I had a crush on, and as much as I knew the young women of the country would love to ogle him, I knew most would be disappointed I'd picked a national hero rather than some teeny bopper singer.

"How about that younger girl? The newer one that always wears the oversized suits? I like that she doesn't give into the stereotype of pop stars. She doesn't sexualize herself, especially since she's so young."

"Frankie Lake?" Carolyn asked.

"Yes, that's her name. Would you please invite her?"

She made a note then handed me the itinerary for tomorrow. "I'm sorry, but you have another suitor arriving tomorrow."

I took the paper from her and frowned until I saw the name. "Peter's coming already?"

She smiled and went back to her folder.

I didn't know when he was arriving. Peter was a childhood friend. We grew up spending every summer together and visited each other through university, but why was he coming as a suitor? If he was interested in me in a romantic way he had every chance in the world to have said something before now. I would have to wait and ask him myself.

A knock sounded on the door and Carolyn answered it. Logan was standing on the other side with a blank expression. I wished he wasn't so good at hiding his emotions. It made it too hard to guess what he was thinking.

"I was wondering if the princess had a moment." He addressed Carolyn but they both looked to me for an answer.

"Of course, please come in." I shared a look with my assistant and she excused herself, leaving me alone with Logan. "Is everything okay?"

He sat across from me and smiled. "Yes, this whole crazy experiment might be over much sooner than expected if you keep up this pace."

I smirked. "I can't say I'm not pleased with the turn of events today."

He ducked his head, staring at the ground. I knew something was bothering him and hoped he would open up to me.

"Logan?"

He rubbed his jaw and finally met my eyes. "There's been something weighing on me lately, and I want to talk to you about it." He sighed. "I don't want to add on to your stress though."

That was concerning. "Please tell me. You're making me nervous."

"I'm sorry." The corner of his lips curled, just barely. "It's about my meeting with my sergeant. I didn't tell you the whole truth."

I sat up. "What happened?"

"He gave me a few options."

"About what?"

"What comes next for me. I can leave active service, retire from duty."

My stomach dropped. He could leave the palace. Leave me.

"I can also continue here in my current position, or he said there's a special task force I have the opportunity to lead. He couldn't reveal too many specifics, but I think it would be out of the country."

I tried not to show my rising panic. "What do you want to do?"

He shook his head. "I'm not sure. I haven't ever given much thought to what I wanted to do after the Marines. I don't know what I could do outside of this."

"You mean a civilian job?"

"I don't have any hobbies outside of training and exercising. I'm not good at very much besides what I do now."

I could sense his turmoil and wanted to help him. "Maybe you just haven't had time to pursue any other interests. You might have other talents you haven't realized yet. What about the task force?"

He shrugged. "I'm not sure I want to commit to several more years."

That was a good sign. He didn't want to leave. It was selfish of me, but I was happy he wasn't leaning toward that option.

"You're amazing at your job and I know there are private security companies that would be lucky to have you on their team, if that's what you want."

He didn't immediately reply. I wanted to tell him to stay, but I couldn't do that to him. If there was another dream he could pursue, I couldn't burden him with my own desires. He should be free to do what he wanted with his life. One of us should.

"I just want you to be happy, Logan. You'll be successful with whatever choice you make."

He stared back at me. "Do you want me here?"

I was taken aback by his directness. "Of course. I don't want you to leave, but that's selfish to say. If there's something else you'd prefer to do, I'd support you. I hope you know that."

He nodded and stood. "Thanks, Isla."

I wasn't sure what he was thanking me for, but I smiled and watched him leave, wondering if there was still something he wasn't telling me.

8

LOGAN

My relief at the quick departure of Count Henri was short lived. Peter, the duke from Denmark and Isla's friend, was arriving anytime, and we just got word that Jean, Count von Hosenbrooke of the Netherlands, was also on his way. He was due this weekend but had moved up his plans which meant my team and the palace staff was working frantically to catch up. In the two years I'd been there I'd never seen Martin, the master of the household, look so frazzled. He was a control freak and perfectionist, which made him excellent at his job, but I worried this was too much for him.

"Peter is on his way." Shane shoved his phone back in his pocket and stood next to me in front of Isla's office. She had the doors open and sat at her desk, staring at her computer screen with a frown. I wanted to call out to her and ask what was wrong, but that would be highly inappropriate.

"Do you have an update on Jean? I thought he was due to arrive first."

He shook his head. "Not since his head of security let me

know their plane was leaving. I thought he would be here by now too, but maybe he isn't coming from home."

I hadn't thought of that. His team didn't mention where they were flying from, so it was hard to estimate when he would land. Maybe his plane would get lost and he'd never show up. That would be too much to ask.

"Are the guests rooms ready?" Carolyn asked a passing maid.

The woman paused her steps. "Yes, ma'am. They were set up to your specifications."

Carolyn grinned and immediately I knew something was going on. Once the maid disappeared down the hall, I took a step closer. "What were your specifications?"

She pursed her lips and looked away. "I simply asked that our guests receive special treatment."

I narrowed my eyes. "And what does that entail?"

She looked to Isla before turning to me. "I told the staff to use new sheets and to be prompt with their wake up calls. A few other minor details."

Shane now stood next to us, tilting his head toward us. "Those new sheets? They wouldn't happen to be the same ones I've heard the maids giggling about?"

She gave nothing away. "How should I know?"

Shane chuckled. "I heard one of them say that they're an all-natural fiber, and the best for the environment, but incredibly scratchy and stiff."

I smirked. "That's one way to make them feel welcome."

"And the wake up calls?" Shane prodded.

Carolyn finally broke. "I have their butlers waking them at five thirty each morning to join Isla for her morning exercise."

I held back a laugh. "But she doesn't exercise until seven or eight, and that's only a few days a week."

She shrugged a shoulder. "We're all willing to make sacrifices at this point."

I glanced over at Isla and smiled. She might not be protesting this directly but she had a plan to drive them crazy.

"And all meals will be completely plant based. No exceptions," Carolyn added with a wink.

This was going to be very interesting. Individually, each change wasn't a big deal, but combined it might just drive a man crazy enough to run him off. I could only hope it had the desired effect.

"Please, let us know how we can help."

She agreed before walking into the office. Shane pulled out his phone and sighed. "Peter is arriving."

We turned together and headed to the main entrance. We stood at the top of the stairs and watched as two black town cars stopped in front of us. Carolyn and Isla came through the open doors and started down to greet Peter.

The moment he stepped out, Isla threw her arms around him and he spun her in the air. I clenched my fist, hating that I didn't have the freedom to do that. I wanted her arms around me, not him. No matter how many times they both repeated that they were only friends, he was here for a purpose. I just needed to figure out what it was.

"Isla, my dear, it's so good to see you." He stepped back from her and took her in from head to toe. "I've missed you."

She beamed up at him like he was the sun, moon, and stars.

I hated it.

"I've missed you, too. Now, let's go inside. We have so much catching up to do."

They breezed past us, and I turned to silently follow. Shane waited for Peter's team so they could coordinate and find their rooms.

Isla led him to her office, and much to my frustration, shut the doors behind her. I wanted to knock or just let myself in. I could claim to be concerned for her safety, but I knew that would be hard to believe. Maybe with any of the other men coming, but not her beloved Peter.

I stared at the doors, trying to break them down with my glare, until I heard footsteps approaching. I glanced to my left to see the queen and her assistant, Marianne, approaching.

I bowed my head just enough; the family didn't require us to formally bow since we were around them so often.

She offered a smile and gestured to the door. "I was told Peter arrived."

"Yes, Your Majesty."

She gave me a stern look. "You know you can call me Anne."

I bit my lip to keep from smiling. If the rest of the country knew how relaxed the royals really were, I doubted they'd believe it. The queen was one of the most regal people I'd ever seen, poised and graceful at all times, but when she was in her own home, without prying eyes, she was just a normal woman and mother.

"They are inside, Anne. Would you like me to announce you?"

She gave me a wry smile. "I don't believe that's necessary." She raised her hand to knock once before opening the doors. She let herself in and instantly beamed. "My dear Peter, you're here."

Marianne shut the door behind them, blessing me with reprieve from having to see their joyful reunion.

It was nauseating.

I had no reason not to like the man, but I did. He claimed to be such a good friend to Isla, but why was he here now?

Why accept the invitation of the king to present himself as a suitor to the princess? It didn't make sense.

Shane marched down the hall. "They're all sorted, and Jean's assistant let me know they will be arriving at the palace just before dinner."

"In time for boiled cabbage?" I said with much satisfaction. "Or perhaps a nice grilled cauliflower steak."

Shane chuckled next to me. "I've never been so happy we don't take our meals with the royal family."

I nodded. At least we wouldn't have to endure Isla's unique form of torture.

"Carolyn sent along a modified schedule for next week. Jean is set to leave on Sunday, Lord Philippe will arrive on Tuesday and leave Thursday, and Lord Marius will be arriving that day. We haven't heard back from Lord Ugyen since she sent him Cian's direct contact information. Perhaps he realized that would be a better way to build a relationship and gain Lochland's support."

"We're down to just three now? I'm surprised more nobles aren't taking advantage of the king's invitation."

Shane checked the hall in both directions before taking a step closer to me and lowering his voice. "I was told Aiden and Cian reached out to their personal contacts and let them know their feelings on it. I believe they scared off most of the potential suitors. They'd be a fool to get on the bad side of the future king."

It didn't come as a shock that Isla's brothers found a way to discreetly take care of things. They loved her and wanted to protect her as much as I did. It was encouraging to know they supported her freedom to choose her future.

We had a few hours of calm before the staff was bustling around again. Jean arrived with much more flourish than Peter. His caravan was eight SUVs long and he emerged like gracing us with his presence was the highest honor. His light brown hair was parted on the side and combed over, which paired perfectly with his starched trousers and sweater. I wasn't sure how he managed to date so many noble women, but maybe he had an appeal I didn't understand.

I watched Isla's reaction and covered my laugh with a cough. She looked disturbed, but hid it well. She was wearing an unfortunately ill-fitting skirt suit that looks like it was made in the nineteen-eighties. Jean met her at the bottom of the steps and bowed slightly before taking her hand and pressing a kiss to it. "It is my greatest pleasure to meet you, Your Highness."

Isla gave him her trained, public smile. "Nice to meet you as well."

Her refusal to use his title was a silent protest I could stand behind.

"Please come in. Dinner will be served soon." Carolyn directed everyone inside while Shane and I watched the stream of men pass us. Once they were inside, Carolyn led them upstairs to the guest quarters while Isla took Jean in the opposite direction toward the portrait gallery. Shane and I followed behind and I remained at the door with the king's head guard, Tomas, while Shane went down to the security room.

This was my chance to ask Tomas if he heard anything about the King's plans, but I had to tread carefully. There were few more loyal to the king.

"An interesting change of pace, no?" I offered as a casual conversation starter.

Tomas raised an eyebrow. "It's certainly causing quite a stir."

That wasn't much to go on, but I had to keep trying. "I heard there were a few suitors who have rescinded their request to attend."

The man merely nodded once.

"Was the King upset by that?"

He gave no reaction. I didn't want to mention Isla's feelings about this whole situation. I knew from what she told me that she made it clear to her parents she wasn't happy nor did she agree with bringing suitors in, but I wasn't sure what the king's staff knew.

"I can't imagine what the count, Jean, can offer the crown or Isla."

Silence was my answer. I waited, hoping he would crack. He knew something. A man in his particular position always had information. Whether or not he felt the need to share it, that was unknown.

"I just want to protect the princess, Tomas."

He swallowed. "His technology company is looking to expand. He wants to build a second headquarters somewhere in Europe. Several countries are courting him to bring his business there. I heard a few Americans are trying to persuade him as well."

"How interesting."

He hummed his agreement.

I wasn't sure if he knew what that bit of knowledge meant for me, or Isla. Surely, Tomas would have kept his mouth sealed if this was a top secret development.

Unless, the king wanted her to find out what was at stake. He knew if Tomas slipped the information to me, I would pass it on. He wanted Isla to offer herself up in exchange for the headquarters? It was too devious, even for the King. I doubted he knew how close his daughter and I were. I was overthinking things.

Which meant he didn't think Isla would find out. Not unless Jean told her himself. What would Isla think of this? Bringing in a company as large as Jean's would mean more jobs for her people. Increased revenue, tourism from employees of the company, and it could push Lochland ahead in the technology race so many countries were fighting in.

It would almost be enough to convince her to sacrifice for the good of her people. I wanted to believe she wouldn't sell herself short. That she would ask Aiden to step in and negotiate a deal that didn't include binding her future to a stranger's.

But if asked, she would do nearly anything for her country. My heart sank.

The moment I got back to the bunks, I would tell Shane what I'd learned. We had to come up with a plan. It might be time for me to tell Shane how I felt about Isla. It was worth the risk to protect the princess.

9

ISLA

Jean was charming. More so than I expected. He was poised and said all the right things. My parents were taken with him. I noticed it the second they walked in how they surrounded him and quickly pulled him into a conversation.

Weren't they concerned by the significant age difference of at least fourteen years? I was two years out of university and he was the owner of a major technology company, established and experienced in life.

I watched him converse with my parents over dinner and wondered if maybe he would be a better fit as a friend for them than a spouse for me. He looked at my father with so much admiration, like a loyal subject. The sight made me lose my appetite. Clearly the man had a mission, and it wasn't me.

Peter, sitting beside me at the dining table, leaned close. "Is he here to get to know you or the King?"

I shot him a look. At least I wasn't the only one who noticed. "I have a feeling I understand this suitor business all a bit more."

His eyebrows rose a fraction. "What do you mean?"

I checked to make sure Jean and my parents were distracted before bowing my head toward him. "He's someone my dad can easily influence. He has something my dad can benefit from. It has nothing to do with me."

Peter's eyes drifted to the far end of the table where my parents invited Jean to sit. "I think you may be right, Isla."

He didn't sound entertained anymore, his voice now held concern.

I dabbed the corners of my mouth and set my napkin in front of my finished dinner plate, hoping to signal the servers to speed things along. Too bad they only cared about my father's pace. They were so caught up in their discussion there wasn't a single complaint about the tofu or chickpeas.

"Why are you here?" As glad as I was to have a visit from my friend. I knew he wasn't here to get to know me or with an interest in marriage. When I asked him earlier he distracted me with tales of his recent travels to South America.

He deflated a bit. "I'm not sure this is the best dinner conversation."

I wanted answers, but I understood the request for discretion. "Do you promise to tell me as soon as we're done?"

He agreed and I found Charlie and Aiden watching us. Aiden's eyes bounced from Jean and back to me before he cocked his head to the side, just slightly.

I rolled my eyes to convey my annoyance. I wasn't positive of Jean's motives yet, but I knew he wasn't here for me any more than Peter was. At the moment, I was quite sick of being used.

Charlie gave me a sad smile. We were only on the entrée course. We still had dessert and drinks to go. I wouldn't be allowed to excuse myself from dinner early, not without repercussions later. My only option was to endure and hope I got some valuable information out of the night.

"Isla, what do you think about that?" Mum asked me and I glanced back to Aiden for help. He shook his head slightly. He wasn't listening either. Wonderful.

"I'm sorry," I replied and Mum's disappointed look made me want to sink into the ground.

"Jean was just telling us about the trip he's going on through southeast Asia. It sounds interesting. Have you ever wanted to travel there?" She gave me a pointed look that said I wasn't allowed to bow out of this conversation.

"Of course. I was able to visit Indonesia and loved it. I would very much like to return and see more of that area."

Jean looked pleased. "Maybe one day, we can see it together."

I forced a smile but the thought made me cringe. "Where is your favorite place to travel?"

See, look Mum. I can participate in a conversation.

Jean stared off to the corner of the room like he was deep in thought. "Petra in Jordan is amazing. Although, if I just want to relax, I prefer Santorini."

I nodded. "I visited Crete."

He hummed. "Another beautiful spot."

With that he angled himself slightly away from me and returned to his conversation with Dad. I wasn't used to being so blatantly dismissed. I almost said something, but decided to let it slide. I could add it to my list of cons about the man.

"That was rude." Peter whispered, and I nodded

"I must not hold his interest." I tried not to sound as bitter as I felt, but I was offended. Why did this man want to waste his time, and my own, by being here when he obviously had no intention of getting to know me? I didn't necessarily want to spend time with him, but I didn't understand. The servers cleared our plates and set small dishes in front of each of us. I smiled down at the raspberry sorbet. My favorite. At least something good came from this night.

Peter took my hand under the table. "You desire to be admired and beloved. No man should be daft enough to ignore you. You should be your husband's equal, not someone he can so easily forget."

I met his eyes and nearly teared up at the sincerity looking back at me. He cared about me and wanted the very best for me, but I knew he wasn't speaking about himself as that husband. What was going on?

Dad waved away the serving staff's offer of coffee and stood from his dining chair. "Jean, would you mind joining me in my office?"

Of course, the man jumped at the opportunity. Without a backward glance, he followed my parents out of the dining hall, leaving me with Aiden, Charlie, and Peter.

"Well, that was interesting," Charlie said with a sympathetic smile.

"Not quite what I was expecting," I agreed.

The doors opened, and Logan stepped in. My heartrate picked up at seeing him, and I fought to keep my reaction under control. I'd never get used to his intimidating stature, and thick muscles. He was a man I knew would always protect me and my heart.

His eyes ran over those of us remaining at the table. He seemed to relax and moved to my side. "May I speak to you, Princess?"

Aiden looked past me. "If it has to do with our guest, please speak freely, Logan."

I twisted in my chair so I could see him, nodding to let him know I was okay with it. He glanced down at Peter cautiously before speaking. "I have a bit of information about the count I think you would be interested in."

"Please, let us know." I urged.

"Jean's company is looking to expand and establish a second headquarters. There are several countries in Europe as well as the US that are courting him to convince him to choose them. It would be a very lucrative move for the country, creating new jobs, boosting the economy, and increasing tourism."

I gasped. It suddenly made so much sense. No wonder he was only interested in speaking with my parents. He wasn't here for me at all, he was here to consider their offer. Was I a part of that? A piece of the bargaining?

Aiden shot out of his seat. "This is ridiculous. I will not let my sister be used in this manner."

Logan nodded. "I was hoping you and your brother might be able to intervene."

"We will. Thank you for letting us know, Logan."

"Of course. I will continue to pass along anything else I discover." He moved to step away, but I reached out and grabbed his hand.

His eyes dropped to mine, holding back the worry but I saw through him. "Thank you."

He gave me a tiny smile before slipping his hand out of mine and exiting the room, leaving us to deal with the bomb he dropped.

"Do you think this kind of thing is only with Jean, or are there more opportunities Dad is considering? Is there something he wants from each of the men?"

Peter shook his head. "I have no company or trade for him."

"You're a family friend and you know how much our mother loves you," Aiden pointed out. "You might be here to throw us off."

Peter looked uncomfortable. "I assure you; I knew nothing of any ulterior plans before I came."

"We know, Peter." I smiled at him. "Would you like to go for a walk with me?"

He stood and helped me from my chair. I turned back to Aiden and Charlie. "I'll see you guys later."

They wished us goodnight and we walked out of the dining hall, passing Logan on our way to the gardens. It was dark out, but I knew the path well. Once we got to the center where the fountain was turned off, we sat on the edge.

"Talk to me, Peter. What's going on?" I'd never seen my friend so resigned. There was something massive weighing on him, and I wanted to help.

"I need to tell you why I'm really here." He paused and I nodded for him to continue. "My parents have been putting pressure on me to settle down and marry as well, but I've resisted for as long as I could. They've been trying to set me up and bring in women for me to court, although, with much more discretion. They tried to play off each visiting woman as though she was merely interested in seeing more of Denmark or visiting a nearby site. Mother would never come out and admit what she was doing."

I took his hand in mine. His voice held so much more pain than I expected from this situation.

"Last month, she grew frustrated. She wants me to marry and produce an heir. She thinks I don't care, and she said she's beginning to lose her patience. When I heard about your father's invitation, I knew it was my chance to get her to back off for a while."

"So, you came to please her?"

He nodded. "That's not all."

What more could he tell me? He wasn't ready to marry. That was fine. I understood why he would take this opportunity to show his mother he was trying.

"I'm not interested in any of the women, Isla. I don't want to marry any of them."

"Okay, you don't have to, Peter. You can wait until you meet the right one."

He sighed and ran his free hand over his face. "It's not that. I'm not interested in women."

I widened my eyes. Oh. Right. I felt horrible I'd made him spell it out so plainly. I should have realized what he was trying to tell me. "Oh Peter. You haven't told your parents?"

He shook his head. "I don't know how. There are no other gay people in the royal and noble community back home."

I nodded. "I don't think there are very many who are openly gay in any of the royal families." I couldn't actually think of any. How alone he must feel. How trapped.

"Peter." I tugged his hand into my lap to pull him closer. His eyes finally met mine and I understood the pain I saw earlier. "I love you no matter what. I want you to know that."

"Thank you, Isla. I was scared you would be mad I was using you, but I'm not ready to tell my family yet. There's still a lot I want to figure out first."

"I understand. You can talk to me anytime. I'll always be here for you."

"Thank you." He leaned over and kissed my cheek. "I'm only here for a few days, but I'll run interference as much as possible."

I smiled. "Thank you."

"Well this is a cozy sight." A voice came from beyond the lit area. Jean slowly emerged looking a bit put out. "I was told Isla was out here. I wasn't aware you were sharing your company with someone else."

Peter stood. "Isla and I were just catching up. I was just going to call it a night, would you mind walking the princess back to the palace?"

Jean nodded, and Peter disappeared. What happened to him helping me? He was abandoning me already.

I shifted as Jean approached and sat next to me. He stayed

a respectable distance away. "I'm sorry I haven't had much of a chance to speak with you. Your parents have been generous hosts."

He had plenty of chances at dinner, he merely chose not to take them. "I'm glad."

"I know there's a bit of an age difference between us, but I want you to know that I sense a maturity about you that I didn't expect. I think we have more in common than either of us know."

I didn't agree in the slightest, but I didn't let him know that. "Like what?"

He smiled. "We both love our countries and our people. We want the best for them, and we want them to prosper."

I nodded. That was true, but it could be said of any royal.

"We're both driven. Me with my company, and you with your philanthropy."

Another broad generality.

"And we both enjoy travel."

Who doesn't?"

"I think the two of us should spend more time getting to know one another, but I'm afraid it will have to be delayed. I have an important meeting that came up, and I have to be in London in the morning."

I couldn't even force a disappointed expression. "Oh no. So soon? You've barely just arrived."

He patted my hand. "I know. It was a brief visit on my part, but I am encouraged by what I saw here." He gave me a pointed look. "I will return as soon as possible."

"Wonderful." I hoped he heard the thinly veiled sarcasm.

He stood, taking my hand to kiss my knuckles. "Please, let me escort you inside."

I wasn't ready to retire quite yet, but I didn't want to risk him prolonging his stay out here with me. I let him help me stand and walked next to him down the stone path to the palace. Once inside, I wished him a good night and hurried down a hall.

He was leaving. I didn't believe he had a meeting mysteriously arise. Either he planned to only stay a few hours from the beginning, or he got the information he needed and didn't want to hang around. Either way I was off the hook.

The moment I was alone, I pulled out my phone and sent a message to Logan letting him know Jean was leaving and thanking him once again for telling me what he found out. It reinforced my feelings for him. He was such a good man.

Why couldn't things in my life be simple for once?

10

LOGAN

"Am I seeing this correctly, Bill?"

He chuckled. "Yes, mate. He's leaving."

I shook my head. I was expecting Jean to be a bigger issue, but he was already leaving the palace. Isla's text shocked me, but the proof was in front of me.

His bags were loaded in his SUV and his team was climbing in. I watched the screen as the parade pulled out and left the gates. Something wasn't adding up. Either the discussion with the king and queen hadn't gone as he hoped and there was no point in staying longer, or it had gone exactly as he planned and there was no reason for him to be around. Maybe it was my own hopes clouding my judgement, but I genuinely couldn't come up with another explanation.

"He can't be giving up that quickly."

"Ey, I'll ask around and see what I can find out. I don't have a good feeling about that one."

I agreed, grateful he said it first. I was suspicious of him and how pure his intentions were, as well as Peter. I couldn't figure him out. Was he just here as a supportive friend? I doubted it. Everyone had something to gain in this, except Isla. She was the one most likely to get hurt. It was my job to keep that from happening. Hopefully letting her and Aiden know about Jean's company would prevent any scheming from happening behind their backs.

"I'll see you in the morning," I called to him as I left the office. We increased the number of guards surveying the grounds now that we had additional guests, but that left Bill alone at night to watch the video feeds. If it was anyone else, I would have insisted I stay with him, but Bill was the best. One of the few I trusted with not only my life, but Isla's.

I got to my room and found Shane resting against the headboard of his bed.

"Jean's gone."

His eyebrows shot up his forehead. "Serious?"

"Yeah, his whole team left."

He shook his head. "There's something off about him."

I filled him in about the information Tomas shared with me.

"So, we know what his real motive is." He sounded relieved. "That's one down and three to go."

"Peter, Lord Philippe, and Lord Marius. Have you found anything else about them?"

"I'm not sure what Philippe has to offer. He's high ranking, but lower than Isla. He's wealthy, but again not more than Isla. I've run background checks and read every article. I can't find anything beyond his time at Oxford. He doesn't have a job or own a company. He seems to be close to the royal family, but other than that, I'm at a loss."

"Maybe he works under a pseudonym."

He straightened. "I've heard of a nobleman who runs estate auctions under a fake name. Another man was a professor, using his mother's name."

"There's no way of finding out." I paused. "Have you run an image check?"

"He didn't appear in anything I could find outside of the expected events and galas."

I nodded and sighed and fell onto my bed.

"We'll figure it out, mate. Don't worry."

I couldn't help but worry. I couldn't let Isla get hurt, let alone stand by while she was forced to marry a man she didn't love. The night passed slowly while I worried over what to do. I slept for maybe three hours total, and it was a relief when my alarm went off early the next morning.

I dressed in shorts and a t-shirt before sliding on my running shoes and heading for the palace gym. It was one of the only places that the royals and staff shared. Since the king and queen never used it, preferring to take walks as their exercise, there was no need for propriety, and all the guards took advantage of the state of the art equipment.

It was often empty when I arrived at five in the morning, but today I was not alone. I stepped in to hear the steady pounding of feet on a treadmill. I moved to the squat rack on the opposite side of the room and let my eyes trail over to investigate. It was Peter. His headphones were in, so he probably wasn't aware of my presence.

Since he was in the zone, and I had no interest in talking, I began my workout as I always did. Thirty minutes later, I was in the middle of my last set of deadlifts when he approached. I pulled out my earbuds when he stopped in front of me.

"I need to talk to you."

I lowered the bar to the ground and stood, waiting.

"I know you and your team are likely investigating me and trying to figure out if I have ulterior motives for being here."

I didn't argue. He was there when I told Isla about Jean's

Her Royal Rebellion | 79

company. He was well aware we were working to protect Isla.

"I want you to know that I already spoke with Isla and told her the truth. I'm not here for courtship or her hand in marriage. I'm here to show my mother I'm trying. She's been pressuring me to marry, and I took advantage of this chance since it was safe. I knew Isla wasn't interested in me, nor I in her."

I narrowed my eyes. "You're not?"

He smirked. "No, she's not my type."

I highly doubted that. He wasn't interested in a beautiful, brilliant, kind woman?

He cleared his throat. "No woman is my type."

Ah. I immediately felt like an idiot. Of course. "Right."

He laughed. "I'm not ready for my family to know, so I'm here to show my Mum that I'm making an effort. Once I figure things out for myself, I'll tell her, but this buys me more time. I wanted you to know that I care about Isla and only want her to be happy. I'm on her side."

"I appreciate you telling me. I'll keep this information to myself, but I'm glad to know you've been honest with her."

"I always will be. She's one of my closest friends. I didn't feel right using her, but I was desperate. While I'm here, I'll do what I can to help figure out the other suitors' agendas. I don't want her hurt any more than you do."

The emphasis he placed on the last two words made me pause. Did he... did he know?

His lip quirked up. "Yeah, I've seen the way you look at the princess. I know how you feel about her."

I looked around, but we were still alone. "It's not appropriate. I'm well aware."

He shook his head. "I wasn't going to say anything like that. I've seen the way she looks at you as well. I think the feelings go both ways, so why haven't you told her?"

My shoulders sagged. "I'm a Marine. Her guard. Not a prince or duke or lord."

"You know as well as I do that none of that matters to Isla."

"It might to her parents. Look who they're trying to set her up with."

He frowned. "Something is going on with them. They've never once told her she was expected to marry a title. I'm not sure what the whole story is quite yet, but I do know that you need to be honest with her. Otherwise, you'll both end up hurt."

With that nugget of wisdom, he walked out of the gym, shutting the door behind him. Not only did he declare himself an ally, but he thought I should tell her how I felt. The one thing that terrified me the most.

I wasn't ready for that, but while I worked on gathering the nerve, I needed to prepare for the next suitor, Lord Philippe, that would be arriving soon.

"He seems normal," Shane muttered over his shoulder as we watched the newest suitor strut down the hallway with Isla on his arm. She looked bored, but at least he was picking up on her cues and showing he had manners.

I disliked the man based on principle, but if I was being objective, he was normal. Almost too much so. Being a noble in Belgium is fairly common. A quarter of their population held a title, so Philippe was less of a commodity there than he was here. I wanted to check in with Isla later tonight to see if he mentioned what he did with his time or his true reason for being here.

All of these new men were making it difficult to find

alone time with her. I missed our stolen moments together. Something had changed the night she broke down in front of me. Holding her felt right. I wished we had a chance to speak again. I longed to tell her about the decision I was facing, but I knew it wasn't the right time. She had more than enough to handle without me adding to her stress.

I returned my attention to the newest guest. From the outside, Philippe was a well-educated, handsome, wealthy lord. He must have a flaw or a secret. If he didn't, I could be in trouble.

As much as I loathed thinking along those lines, I had to begin accepting my situation. I wanted Isla to be happy, no matter what. If that meant she ended up with him, I would have to find a way to be okay with it. It would make my career decision easier at least. I'd be able to take the special task assignment without anything holding me back.

I didn't want that to be a default decision. If I was only willing to consider it if Isla turned me down, then maybe that was all I needed to know. I wasn't interested in it. Not enough to commit for an unknown time at an unknown location.

Well, that was one major decision off my chest. I was left with two options. Leave active service or stay?

My eyes found Isla. It all depended on her. As unfair as it was to put that on her, it was the truth, even if she was unaware.

"Did you talk to the maids?" I asked quietly as we paused outside of Isla's open office door. She sat inside, chatting with Philippe and Carolyn.

"Yes, they will remain vigilant. None of them have heard anything from the king or queen to help us, but I doubt their personal staff would reveal anything. They're annoyingly loyal."

He rolled his eyes, and I chuckled. "How horrible that they have integrity."

"Hey, we're all on the same team. Everyone here wants the princes and princess to be happy. We all love them. Expect those who serve the king and queen. They think they're above everyone else."

I shook my head. Even within the palace staff there was a social hierarchy and cliques.

"At least we can depend on those serving the suitors to spill it all."

He grinned wickedly. "Oh yes. They love gossiping about them. So far, I learned that Peter's nighttime skin routine lasts over thirty minutes and that he only sleeps on silk pillow cases."

I smirked. "I'm sure the princess would love to tease him about spending more time than her on his skin routine, but that isn't really enough to get him sent on his way."

He shrugged. "No, but it means they're watching closely. I thanked them and told them to find me with anything else they discover."

"I'm sure they loved that." More than a couple of the maids had expressed their interest in Shane, but he remained aloof. Giving them a reason to track him down and talk to him was like dangling a bone in front of a dog. Of course, they would jump at the chance.

"When all of this is over, we should take a day off and indulge in a day of golf." He had a far-off look in his eye and I quickly agreed.

"I could certainly be talked into that."

He seemed pleased by the idea. During stressful times while deployed and living in less than ideal conditions, my men and I would come up with dreams and ideas of what we would do when we got back home. Some days it was as simple as drinking ice cold water and lounging in a soft chair. Other days we thought about racing cars or lavish vacations. It was all we needed to push through particularly tough times.

My job now wasn't anywhere near as bad as it used to be, but we still needed something to look forward to. A goal to distract us from the monotony of the day to day.

"There's a great course near Taramore I've always wanted to play," I added.

He nodded, and Isla stood and led the group back to the hall. She held my gaze while she passed, heading off toward the east exit. We waited a beat before trailing them.

Sometimes it was a stolen glance or secret smile that got me through my days. When she looked at me like that, like I was someone special or important to her, it was enough to keep my heart full of hope. It was all I needed to watch other men touch and talk to her. They might have her attention now, but they could never know her like I did.

11

ISLA

Philippe was by far the least offensive of the men who had arrived, but that was like saying he's the kindest lion. He was still a threat to me and my future. Perhaps if we were meeting under any other circumstances, I'd give him an honest chance, but I couldn't. My guard was up, and I wasn't letting any of these men close to me, emotionally or physically.

"Are you sure you like this option best?" Silvia, my dressmaker, was frowning behind me in the mirror.

"It's perfect." My parents decided to throw a ball this evening so I could continue to get to know Peter, Philippe, and the last man who was expected to arrive sometime today. I knew nothing of Lord Marius, none of my friends throughout Europe did either. He was a mystery, and while some would find that exciting or appealing, I was suspicious.

My parents expected me to play nice with the guests and dance around the ballroom like I was having the time of my life. I knew better than to try to get out of it, so I decided to control what little I could.

"It's just so different for you." She tugged on the long,

billowy sleeve. "You have such lovely shoulders and arms."

The lace overlay of the dress was exactly what I wanted. I loathed the idea of men I don't like or know touching me. I didn't want my back exposed like I normally did. I didn't even want them touching my wrist without my permission and now they couldn't. At least, not my bare skin.

The cream lace was accented with a pale pink bow that pulled in at the waist and tied in the back, and matched the color of the underlayer. It was pretty. Modest. Definitely not something I would wear normally, but this ball was far from normal.

"I love it."

She gave in and began pinning areas that needed to be taken in or hemmed. "You'll look lovely. The men won't know what to do with themselves."

I smiled to myself. Hopefully they would be distracted by all of my surprise guests.

My parents might think they had the upper hand since they sprung the ball on me just last night, but they underestimated how loyal my friends were. I sent one mass text to my wonderful girls, and now a dozen of the most beautiful and eligible women in Europe would be attending tonight.

They knew and understood the situation I was in better than nearly anyone else could. They wanted me to have the ability to choose my future myself and agreed to come and steal the attention of any man I didn't want near me. They would be too tempting to ignore, especially if the men were only after a titled, attractive woman rather than me.

Only Logan, Shane, and my maids knew of the incoming guests. Since they weren't planning to stay in the castle overnight, I didn't need to have rooms prepared. I simply let my few closest maids know to expect a few more people tonight so they could pass along the message to the kitchen and staff preparing the ballroom.

"That's all, love. I will get this finished and back to you this afternoon." Silvia stood and helped me out of the dress, careful not to move a pin.

"Thank you." I slid on my robe and walked her out.

Once she was gone, I hurried to dress. I wanted to catch Aiden and Charlie before they were caught up in meetings for the day. I stepped out of my room and smiled at Shane. He nodded once and followed silently behind me as I strode down the hall. I made it to the main staircase when my name was called.

I froze and looked around. Philippe was in front of the main entrance watching me. "I'm so glad I found you. I was hoping to spend some time together before tonight."

I wanted to sigh and run back to my room, but escape was not an option. "I'll have to check my schedule for the day. I might be full until the ball."

"No, miss. You're available all day. Your father saw to it himself that all your meetings were moved or your brothers will be attending in your place." I glanced over my shoulder to see Carolyn staring down at her folder like she was hiding from me. Impeccable timing for her to show up.

"Lovely." I did little to hide my sarcasm. She was supposed to be on my side. I couldn't completely fault her though. The king was the boss.

"Wonderful. How does a ride sound?" His face was so full of hope. I wanted to crush it then and there.

"Can you give me a few minutes? I have to change first." I gestured to my navy dress, and his grin widened.

"Of course. I will meet you at the stables."

I nodded and turned to head back to my room. "You've got to be kidding me."

Shane chuckled behind me.

I glared at him before cracking and shaking my head.

"The Americans have rubbed off on you," he added.

I couldn't deny it. I'd picked up on a few of their sayings and mannerisms. I knew it bothered my parents, but at this point I was ready to walk into my father's office and demand to know if he'd lost his mind.

I changed into a pair of white riding pants, boots, and a tan sweater before my second attempt to head downstairs. I took the long way through the halls, pausing near Dad's door. It was shut and I heard voices, so I moved on to Mum's drawing room. She was sitting next to her assistant and they both glanced up when I entered.

Mum ran her eyes over my outfit and smiled. "What a wonderful day for a ride."

I narrowed my eyes. Did she have something to do with Philippe's invitation? Did she make the suggestion to him?

"Why was my schedule cleared?"

She remained poised and unaffected despite my attitude. "Your father and I felt your time would be better utilized this week spending time getting to know the guests that have arrived just to meet you."

"I have projects I'm working on. The Independence Day celebration is weeks away. I can't just push everything to the side."

She gave me a gentle smile. "Darling, your team can manage everything without you."

"So, I'm just a pretty face for the public? My ideas and work don't actually matter?"

I was wearing on her patience but her control was better than mine. "Of course not. I'm simply stating that you have excellent people appointed on each project that are more than capable of running things for a few days without you. I'm sure if there is anything that needs your attention, Carolyn will let you know."

She looked to my assistant who instantly nodded. "Of course, Ma'am."

Fine. I was outnumbered and overpowered. "Fine. If anyone needs me, I'll be off somewhere alone with a complete stranger."

Mum gave me a patronizing smile. "Your guards will always be nearby, and Philippe is a gentleman."

That confirmed my suspicion that she was somehow behind this. I never mentioned who I was going riding with.

I sighed and left without another word. Shane looked like he was trying not to laugh, and he'd better not lose that battle. He was one of the few people I could take my anger out on without repercussion. Carolyn might cry, and my maids would ask to be transferred. Even Logan would make me talk about why I was feeling a certain way, but Shane would simply let me get it all out, maybe even let me punch his shoulder a few times and then walk away.

The idea was tempting.

"One word," I threatened and his lips pursed.

"Just one thing. Logan will be joining you for the ride. I have ... an assignment."

I narrowed my eyes. "How did you get out of it?"

He twisted his lips before a smile broke through. "I traded a night shift."

I rolled my eyes and headed down to the stables and I prayed this would be a quick outing. At least I could blame the ball if it dragged out. Phillippe didn't need to know how quickly I was able to get ready. I could take hours upon hours for all he knew.

"There you are." Philippe emerged from a stall with a wide smile. He was an expressive man who didn't bother to hold back his emotions. It would be endearing if I had made his acquaintance under any other circumstance.

"Hello. Has Joseph set you up with a horse?" I looked around for our stable hand who cared for our animals.

"Yes, I'll be riding Parsley. He said that's Cian's horse but he's the most welcoming to new people."

That wasn't entirely true. Parsley was a bit temperamental and didn't like inexperienced riders. I smiled. I'd be by with a tray of Joseph's favorite chocolate biscuits later.

"Wonderful. I'll just get Jasmine ready." I moved to my pure white Irish Sport. She was bred for show jumping, but wasn't a very good student so a family friend gifted her to me when I was sixteen. We both preferred easy, slow rides and became a perfect match. Aiden and Cian enjoyed racing and challenging each other on their horses, but Jasmine and I were more dignified than that. Another surprise for Philippe. Parsley was used to taking off for the woods and racing Steel, Aiden's horse.

Logan appeared giving me a discrete wink before moving down to the last stall where Jerry, our Irish Draught, waited. Jerry was an older, more docile horse. One that our guests usually rode. He was patient and forgiving. If I was a kinder person, I would have insisted Philippe ride him.

Oh well.

Jasmine was ready and waiting for me, munching on a bucket of apples. I took her reins and led her outside before slipping my foot into the harness and pulling myself up. I waited for Philippe and Logan to join me while patting her silky neck.

"We're not going to be out too long, okay?" In my mind she always understood me perfectly. She knew when I just needed time away from everyone and we would take long, lazy walks through the woods. I rarely directed her, simply letting her wander where she wished, carrying me along for the adventure. "Tell Parsley to take it easy too. I don't want anyone hurt today."

She turned her head toward me and I swear she smiled. Horses were smart creatures with their own personalities. I swear she was laughing along with me.

The men walked their horses out and I got a few minutes to giggle while Philippe struggled to mount Parsley. Each time he put his foot in the harness, Parsley took a few steps, just enough to make Philippe lose his balance and jump back. It happened three times before Logan jumped down and held Parsley in place long enough for Philippe to settle into the saddle.

"Ready then?" Philippe had the grace to chuckle at himself.

"Sure." I tapped my heels against Jasmine's sides and she started her slow, steady jaunt down the path to the woods.

"Whoa there." I heard Philippe call out a few times, but I remained faced forward. Let Logan worry about the poor man. I was being a horrible host, but any show of concern would only encourage him.

"Pull back, sir," Logan called out.

"I'm trying." Philippe's voice held panic. "He's not listening."

I glanced over as he passed me with a death grip on the reins. Parsley was only trotting, but I could tell the horse was growing impatient. By this time, Cian would have disappeared from view.

I checked over my shoulder and Logan gave me a tiny smile. He was enjoying this as much as me.

"Maybe just let him trot. We'll stay behind you." I offered.

Philippe gave me a stiff nod and relaxed his hold. The horse took that as his signal and took off at a run down his favorite path. To his credit, Philippe looked like an experienced rider, but he wasn't a match for the stubborn horse.

"Come on. Let's not fall too far behind." I encouraged Jasmine to follow and she sped up just a bit. Philippe never disappeared from view, but I could see his frustration in his raised shoulders. He wasn't enjoying this leisurely ride.

"How are you doing?" Logan asked.

It was the first time in a while that someone asked. I glanced at him and attempted a smile. "I'm trying to stay optimistic."

He nodded. "Hopefully we can continue to scare them away."

I almost laughed. "We have gotten quite lucky."

He winked and I nearly swooned. "Are you sure we can't just run away?"

He ducked his head and slowed Jerry. I took that as a no and urged Jasmine forward.

"Should I go round him up?" Logan offered from behind me.

I nodded. "It's only going to make Parsley angrier the longer they ride."

I slowed Jasmine down and we enjoyed a quiet walk while Logan and Jerry surged ahead to catch up to the lord.

"I don't think he's going to be very pleased when he gets back," I leaned forward and told Jasmine while I stroked her mane. Her head bounced in agreement and I giggled.

I let the men figure things out and turned Jasmine down a short path that circled back to the stables. The sun cut through small breaks in the trees, providing just enough warmth for me not to chill. The calm around me was a tease. I longed to spend the rest of the day out here but I would be found in minutes. As soon as Mum or Dad saw a suitor without me, they'd send out a search party since that was all I existed for at the moment.

I still couldn't believe my father had gone so far as to clear my schedule without even warning me first. Was I really so dispensable? No one on any of the committees needed me? Things would move forward seamlessly without my presence. Why did I bother then?

I thought they were proud of me for being involved. I could spend my days traveling, shopping, or enjoying the company of my friends. I could overindulge in the privileges my life had to offer, but no. I was responsible. I wanted to help and make a difference. Why didn't they see that? Why was I just a future trophy wife to them?

That had me smirking. Mum would fall over if I said that to her, but it was one of my favorite Charlie-isms. Every time she said it, I thought of a small gold figurine frozen in place with a fixed smile, forever on a pedestal. It didn't sound all that far off from my life, well a life with one of these men. They didn't want me. They wanted the Princess of Lochland. Why didn't my parents see that?

Did I not deserve more than that?

I froze as the white stable came back in view. Did they not think I should have more out of life than a loveless marriage based on money and titles? Didn't my happiness matter?

I couldn't believe my parents would be that heartless, but that's how it looked right then.

The idea stung, but I couldn't fixate on it.

"Isla, there you are!" Joseph called out. "Marius is arriving. You're needed back at the palace immediately." I groaned.

As I got closer, he met me and helped me off Jasmine before taking her reins. "Thanks for letting me know. Logan and Philippe are still out there. Would you mind letting them know where I went when they get back?"

He nodded once. His tan skin was lined with wrinkles that shifted as he smiled. "Can't imagine they had any problems."

I grinned and shook my head. "You're a clever man, Joseph. I won't forget that.'

He winked and led my horse back inside while I took the path to the palace.

12

LOGAN

"So, it's safe to say Philippe isn't a contender?" Shane asked as we rounded the corner to a better position in the ballroom.

"You should have seen it. You would have fallen off your horse."

I chuckled, thinking about how the Belgium man attempted to romance the princess and ended up embarrassing himself. She even left before I returned to the stables with the disgraced Philippe. The lord wasn't all that happy about getting left behind with her guard, but I doubted very much that Isla cared.

She looked beautiful, but unlike herself, in her gown. The ballroom was full of Lochish nobles and the family's friends. I recognized several faces, but there were a handful of young women who I only vaguely recognized from pictures in Isla's room. These must be the friends she called to come in and act as distractions.

When she told me and Shane what she'd done in response to her father's announcement of the ball, I wanted to pick her up and hug her. She was a genius. Her parents couldn't get upset that she invited her closest and most trusted friends to come meet the men who were pursuing her.

Of course, Isla's friends were doing much more than that. They were acting as very discrete barriers between the princess and the various men who wanted to speak to her. She was currently sipping a bubbly drink and chatting with Charlie at a small table on the outskirts of the room. No one could say that she wasn't trying or making herself available. She smiled and greeted the guests, but the men just happened to be occupied with her very determined friends.

"Watch this one." Shane tilted his head in the direction of a tall brunette wearing a gold ball gown. She was stunning, and seemed to have Philippe under her spell. Every time he glanced in Isla's direction, the brunette would side step, blocking him and ensuring his attention remained on her.

The downside of being a well-bred noble was the standard of impeccable manners. He couldn't very easily excuse himself or risk offending a young, beautiful, powerful woman. If this was who I thought it was, the king of Spain would not appreciate Philippe disrespecting his youngest daughter.

I let a small smile slip. "He's in quite a precarious situation."

"And Marius is stuck as well."

I scanned the room for the dark haired man. He stood out among the crowd with his slightly unruly appearance. He had a long, full beard and wore a flashy white, silk tux. Two of Isla's friends were occupying him, but he wasn't making nearly as much of an effort to pretend to be interested. His eyes stayed on Isla and he was slowly shifting so his back was to her. In a few more minutes he'd have an unobstructed path to the princess. He was clever.

The moment I laid eyes on him this afternoon, something in my gut put me on alert. He didn't say or do anything suspicious. He wouldn't still be around if he was that obvious, but this was more than me simply not liking a man that was here for the woman I cared about. No, this was my military training kicking in and telling me to watch carefully.

"See what he's doing?" I asked quietly.

Shane didn't respond immediately, but eventually caught on. "He's moving them without their notice. He's going to be able to quickly excuse himself and get to Isla in just a few more moments."

I nodded as we watched exactly what he predicted unfold. There wasn't anything we could or should do to stop it. As long as we were paying attention to the rest of the room and there was no threat to the princess, we were to remain unnoticed.

Isla looked up from Charlie when Marius approached them. I watched her forced, fake smile appear, then Charlie stood and left them alone. Isla shifted so her legs were folded away from him, and she leaned back in her seat, creating as much distance between them as possible. Was he not picking up on her body language? It screamed to leave her alone.

He continued talking to her, undeterred. She gave brief responses and her eyes roamed the area, probably looking for an escape. What were all of those friends doing? When her gaze met mine, I saw the plea. She wanted an interruption. She wanted me to come over, but I couldn't. I knew my place. Unless she was in danger, I couldn't simply walk up and ask for her to leave the man. That would raise more than a little suspicion.

My heart was breaking at her pained expression. I could only pray she knew how badly I wanted to be there for her. If things were different, I never would have let him within ten feet of her, but I had to remember who I was and more importantly who she was.

"She looks miserable," Shane said with a sigh.

I agreed. "Why isn't anyone saving her?"

I wanted to be that person, but right now she needed one of her friends. I looked for any of the women, but didn't see them. "Where are they?"

Shane took a small step forward. "I'm not sure. I'm going to go check. Something feels off."

He turned and walked away while I remained focused on the princess. His suspicion only encouraged mine. The other guards weren't outfitted with headsets or mics, so I couldn't share my concern or check with Shane on his status. We only used those in public, but maybe it was time for a change. It had never been an issue at previous events, the guest lists and security screens made sure we heard of any threats. Tonight felt different.

My attention was diverted when Marius stood and offered his hand to Isla. I could see the hesitation in her face from across the room, but without anyone stepping in she stood and he led her to the dance floor. Where were her friends?

What was the point of having them here if they disappeared in her true time of need? If Shane told me they got distracted by someone or something short of a life or death situation, I would personally escort each of them off the palace grounds.

Isla and Marius merged in with the other couples on the dance floor, and I could no longer clearly see Isla. I made my way around the room for a better position. I was almost to the table they'd just vacated when Shane caught up to me.

"They were told Prince Aiden needed them immediately." He turned his back to the crowd so they couldn't see his reactions.

"And what did he need with them?"

"That's the thing. They couldn't find him, and when I

finally tracked him down, he had no idea what I was talking about."

I kept my face expressionless. "Who told the women they were needed?"

"One of the servers."

"Did you find out who?" I was growing frustrated.

"Yes. It was a newer employee and when I questioned him, he said one of the guests passed on the message. He pointed them out. It was a parliament member. When I questioned him, he said a man that said he was friends with Aiden was looking around and he offered to help. He pointed him out in the crowd, and it was Marius."

I shook my head. That was a long trail to follow, too long to be a misunderstanding. "That was planned."

"I agree. He went to great lengths to hide his identity."

"Maybe he just wanted a chance to talk to Isla." I was playing devil's advocate even though my mind was practically screaming at the red flags.

"It's possible, but if anything, it just puts a bigger target on his back." I was glad Shane was just as concerned. Sometimes my personal feelings made me question whether or not I was allowing them to cloud my judgement. Good to know I wasn't there yet.

The women filed back into the room and spread out, but it was too late. Unless one of them asked to cut in, Marius had Isla to himself.

I noticed one lovely redhead with her eyes locked in our direction. "You've gained a fan."

Shane turned and his eyes immediately found her. "Oh yes, Enya is quite a catch. She was the only one to offer to help me track down the truth of what happened. She marched right up to the parliament member and questioned him. It was a sight."

I chuckled. "Perhaps you should get her contact information before she leaves, in case you have any follow up questions."

He nodded and seemed to consider it. "That would be the best course of action. I wouldn't want to let anything slip between the cracks."

I smiled and shook my head. I wasn't sure who Enya was or how she knew Isla, but I knew she wasn't a royal at least. Probably the daughter of a duke or a friend from Isla's university days. Hopefully she and Shane could find a way to continue to get to know one another. They were obviously very attracted to one another. I sighed. If only it was that simple for me.

Watching another man with his hands on Isla's shoulder and waist, knowing it was likely I'd never have that opportunity, was like a hot knife puncturing my stomach. The only thing keeping me sane was her uncomfortable expression and the way she held herself away from him. It was enough for me to know she wasn't enjoying this. She probably wished, even more than me, that she was out of his grasp.

Even though I wanted her to be happy and find someone she could have the life she deserved with, it would kill me to stand back and watch it all happen. If I were a better man, I might be able to silently support her, but I knew it would be the hardest thing I'd ever have to endure. It would likely be the thing to push me over the edge. I'd have to ask for reassignment, or leave active service. A tiny part of me wished for her to fall for someone else, just to end my misery. She could make my decision for me.

But I knew in my heart my feelings weren't completely one sided. There was more than just feelings of friendship between us. She didn't think of me as just her guard. The way she treated Shane and acted around him was different from me. She was kind and friendly to him, but she was less formal to me. Her walls were lowered. She told me things she didn't share with anyone else.

She told me when I first was assigned to her that her parents had the perfect love story. They grew up with each other and gradually fell in love. She wanted that. She wanted a marriage that lasted, and most importantly, she wanted a life full of passion and love. One night, I checked on her to catch her trying to hide a book beneath a sofa pillow. Between her quick movement and red face, I knew she was up to something. I teased her and made weak attempts to remove the pillow until she caved. She pulled out a thick binder and showed me the pictures she'd gathered to plan her ideal wedding. There was page after page of wedding gowns. Some from runways and others from past royal weddings. She had visions of the flowers, cathedral, and even centerpieces. I sat with her for over an hour as she explained each page. She had everything picked out and coordinated. She knew exactly what she wanted and joked that all she needed now was her dream man. The way she looked at me that night... I think that's when I realized how I felt about her. When our eyes met it was like something clicked in my heart.

I couldn't imagine how devastated that girl would be if she knew what her father had planned for her.

I shook my head. I wasn't willing to give up yet.

No, I couldn't just walk away until I knew for certain that there was never going to be a chance for us. As long as I knew there was a sliver of hope, I wouldn't abandon her. I'd be her rock, her shoulder to cry on, her confidant until she told me to leave.

I straightened my shoulders, more confident than I'd felt in days. I knew what I wanted. Maybe not with my profession, but I knew my heart.

13

ISLA

Nerves made my chest tighten but I forced myself to pull my shoulders back and smile. I swung open the door and Logan glanced up from his position outside my room. His smile made my entire body relax. One look from him and I felt right.

"Good morning, Princess." His eyes trailed up and down my body and I felt my cheeks warm. I enjoyed when he slipped and let me see he saw me as more than his assignment. "What do you have planned today?"

I was wearing fitted pants and a thick maroon sweater. "A mission."

His eyebrows rose. "Oh really?"

I nodded and headed down the hall toward the back staircase that would lead outside. The sound of his boots on the marble made me smile. He was the only person in my life that didn't ask questions, didn't try to talk me out of something, or control me. He simply followed.

Once we were outside, he stayed half a step behind me, but I could watch him out of the corner of my eye. He looked a little worn out. I felt responsible for his added stress and duties, but it was my parents' fault. He was working nearly eighteen-hour days, instead of trading shifts with Shane and the night guard. He was with me all day. I knew he was worried about my safety with all these strangers in the palace, but I couldn't help but hope he was doing it to keep the men in line as well. That he cared enough to make sure they didn't have the opportunity to be alone with me.

As we crossed through the garden and toward the lake, out of sight of the palace staff, he moved closer to me. "Do I get a hint as to what we're doing?"

I smiled, not having to fake it for the first time in days, and pointed. "You're going to help me."

He followed the direction to the two targets I had set up. "Archery isn't exactly my specialty."

His voice held humor and a bit of nerves. I liked that I was able to make my solid, stalwart guard nervous.

"Well, I haven't picked up a bow in almost ten years, and I was hoping to show off when Serena gets back."

He turned to me. "Do you have some bet going on that I don't know about?"

"Not exactly. I just know she's going to come back from training thinking she's the toughest of us, and I want to make sure I can still best her at something."

He started laughing and looked down at the bow next to mine. "I'm more of a rifle man, but I think I remember enough to use this."

He picked it up and expertly held it against him. He looked like Apollo, poised and completely comfortable.

"Looks like you know exactly what you're doing." I didn't bother trying to hide my perusal of his body. The muscles in his arms flexed and bulged as he raised the bow in front of him and pulled back the string.

He caught me and winked before bending over to select an arrow. He placed it on the arrow rest and pushed the nock onto the string before pulling his arm back, taking only a few seconds to aim before releasing the arrow.

"Dead center." I clapped and he smiled. "Now teach me your ways."

He set his bow down and grabbed mine, lifting it into position and directing my hands. "Move this hand up a bit." He nodded. "Now pull here." He guided my hand until my thumb grazed my face. His eyes locked on mine and felt the heat between us grow.

"Like this?" I whispered.

His eyes trailed down to my lips, staring. "Yes."

I lowered the bow and lifted my head toward him. I knew what he was thinking. What he wanted. It was the same thing I did. No one was around. No one would know. I waited for him to react, to take the lead. Time froze as he leaned forward. This was it. The moment I'd thought of and hoped for.

"I can't." Logan took a step back with sorrow in his eyes.

"Why?" My voice came out in a gasp. "Why not?"

I saw the plea in his expression for me to understand, but I refused to give up this time.

"Isla, I can't be with you."

"That's not true. We can try. We can talk to my parents and your commander. We can find a way."

His hand came up and his fingers brushed my face. "I want to be with you more than anything. It physically hurts to see you with anyone else, but Isla, I have nothing to offer you. I can't provide what these other men can. How can I go to your father and ask for permission when you have so many better options?"

"You mean men that are here for every reason but wanting to get to know me? Men that only see me as a means to an end?" He was finding excuses. "The only thing that should matter is how we feel for each other."

"I agree, but that's not the world we live in."

"Logan, please." I can count on one hand the number of times I've had to beg in my life, but I would get on my knees and grovel if it meant he understood how much he meant to me. "I can't live a life without you in it. Surely my parents will see that and understand. I wouldn't care if you're penniless, but that's not the case. You're a well-respected, decorated Marine. You've dedicated your life to serving our country, as I have. That matters." I could see his resolve wavering. He was considering it. "Please, Logan."

His chest rose as he took in a deep breath.

"Princess," a voice called from behind us, and I nearly cursed the intruder. I turned and frowned when I realized it was Marius. What was with this guy? He was like a leech. He'd hovered over me at the ball until the moment I excused myself and ran for the sanctuary of my room. Every attempt at diversion or talking to someone else was a fail. He was always there, waiting.

"Marius, what are you doing out here?" I didn't bother sounding pleasant. He was uninvited and ruining one of the most important moments of my life.

"I was looking for you, of course. One of the butlers mentioned he saw you headed this direction."

I would have to hunt down that particular man and let him know it was not his responsibility, nor his right, to share my location with strangers.

Fine. I was being irrational. The staff hardly knew how to distinguish between people that were and were not privileged to know of my whereabouts. If anything, Father told them to assist the new guests in any way possible.

"What can I do for you?"

His gaze flickered to Logan before returning to me. "I wasn't aware you were a fan of archery."

"There's much you don't know about me."

The fool continued to approach me. "I'm a fairly skilled archer. I could show you some pointers."

"Thanks, but my guard is more than capable of teaching me."

He nodded and slid his hands in his pockets. "Perhaps I might have a moment alone with you? I am here to get to know you, after all."

"I should be done within the hour. I can find you then."

His expression darkened. "Isla, with all due respect, I've traveled quite far to meet you. I only have a few days to spend with you and I would appreciate it if you would make the time now. Your lesson can be rescheduled for another time."

My frustration was growing. "I'm well aware of your sacrifices to be here, but you must also respect my time. If I feel that my presence is needed here at the moment then you need to accept that. I will be with you shortly."

His eyes narrowed for only a second. I caught it, and I wondered if Logan did. "Fine. I will wait."

He took a single step back and folded his hands behind him, watching. Did he think this was the way to win me over? Challenging me and trying to exert pressure on me? He might be stubborn but he had nothing on me.

I turned back to the targets. "Now what?"

Logan was glaring over my shoulder and took a few seconds to return his attention to me. "I can't believe him."

"Ignore him." I picked up the bow and lifted it like he showed earlier. "Now what?"

He grabbed an arrow and put it in place. "Now look down the arrow and align it with the center of the target."

His hand gently rested on mine, helping me get closer to my goal. "When you're ready, release."

I took in a breath and as soon as I was sure, released the

arrow and exhaled. It shot forward and hit the first ring, just inches away from my goal.

I smiled and looked up to see Logan beaming. "That was great."

"Thanks." I lowered the bow and focused on the true purpose of bringing him here. "You're a really great teacher, very patient."

He shrugged. "I've had to do a lot of training over the years."

"Do you enjoy it?"

He seemed to think about it. "I do, actually."

Perfect. That was easier than I expected. "Then we figured out an option."

His eyebrows pulled together. "What do you mean?"

"We know something you like. Something you're passionate about. Maybe you could be some sort of trainer or instructor. I'm not saying a traditional school teacher, but something active or outdoors."

After a few seconds he began nodding. "You're right. That's a really good idea." His eyes locked on mine. "Thank you."

I wanted to hug him or touch him in any way, but Marius was still close. I could feel his stare. "We can keep exploring options like this. We'll find the right fit."

"Do you want to keep practicing and make him wait a while more?" His wicked grin almost made me laugh.

"Of course."

We spent another ten minutes shooting, and I finally hit center, once.

"Well done, Princess," Marius said. He'd moved close behind me. "Now that you've proven yourself, may we speak?"

I lowered the bow, tempted to aim my next shot at him. I faced him again. "Patience is not a virtue you possess, I see."

He chuckled. "Can't say I've had to practice it often in my life."

And that made him all the less attractive.

"Marius, I don't appreciate your behavior or attitude. Quite frankly, after your display last night and this morning, I have no interest in getting to know you or spending another second in your company. There's no reason for you to wait for me to finish. I will not be bossed around by any man, let alone some lord from a country I know nothing about. You have been rude, possessive, and you obviously forget your place. I am the princess. You're excused."

I turned away and raised the bow, hitting center once again. I wanted to cheer but didn't want to break from my epic display of power and composure. After a moment, Logan relaxed and I knew the vile man was gone.

"Wow. I don't know what to say. That was remarkable." Logan was shaking his head.

I sighed and placed the bow on the ground. "I can't believe I said all of that, but I couldn't take it anymore. I'm so sick of men forgetting who I am. I cannot be pushed around or controlled. I won't allow it."

"I'm so proud of you."

My chest swelled at the compliment and I felt like I was soaring, until I heard my father call my name.

I sighed and turned back to Logan. "I'll see you later." I didn't know what my father wanted, but I had a feeling it wasn't going to be good news.

14

LOGAN

Isla inspired me in more ways than one. Not only did she stand up for herself and put that idiot Marius in his place, but she figured out something about me that I wasn't even aware of. It meant so much to me that she took the time to help me. I knew she cared about me and wanted me to be happy, but this proved it.

There was more than just hope that she might feel the same about me. She was willing to go to her parents. She wanted to fight for our chance to be together. I was trying to be realistic and not get ahead of ourselves, but my heart was so full.

She showed me it was okay to dream big. After she walked away, I went straight to my desk to list more ideas that I can explore. I might not be an expert in archery, but I knew quite a bit about self-defense, security, and leadership. I chuckled at the idea of being a public speaker, one of the ideas that the internet suggested when I searched leadership positions. People wanted to hear from war heroes and those who'd overcome the impossible. I was neither. Plus, public speaking was not one of my strengths. I doubted the front row would appreciate me spewing on them when I walked on stage.

Give me a tank or rifle and I was ready to go, but a small crowd was enough to make my knees buckle.

"What are you doing?" Shane walked in wearing a towel around his waist. He was able to sneak away for a few hours today to spend more time with Enya, while I covered his post, but now I wanted answers.

"I'll tell you after you tell me." I wagged an eyebrow earning a laugh from him.

"I'm not doing anything interesting. I'm simply getting to know a nice young woman."

"Oh yeah? And what did you learn today?"

He pulled on a shirt and sat on the edge of his bed. "That I really, really like her. She's brilliant, Logan. She's getting a doctorate in microbiology. She's going to cure some disease I swear." He smiled and shook his head. "I have no idea why she's interested in a dumb guy like me, but she is."

"Where does she live?" I could already see where this was going. Shane was a diligent, dedicated Marine but I'd seen that faraway look enough over the years to know he was checking out.

"Tarramore. She's attending university there." He was so excited.

"So, when will you let Sergeant Brown know?"

His brows pulled together. "What are you talking about, mate? I'm not leaving."

"Sure, you are. I've seen enough men in love to know what's coming next."

He laughed. "I'm not in love."

"Yet." I sighed. "I'm happy for you. I knew this was going to happen eventually. Can I just ask that you don't do anything until we can get things with the princess settled?"

"Logan, mate, I swear I'm not going anywhere. Besides,

aren't things already settling? Peter and Philippe are the only ones left, and I saw the Belgium looking quite cozy with one of Isla's friends tonight. I don't see him staying around much longer."

"This isn't over, not for the king. You don't really think he'll give up after one round of suitors."

Shane's face dropped. "You're right. I shouldn't have thought it would be so easy."

"That's why I need you around, at least until Isla can convince her parents to stop this madness. Then you can run off with your love."

He threw a pillow at me, but I hit it to the ground and laughed. "Now will you tell me what you're doing?"

"Ah yes. Isla asked me to help her with her archery. Afterward she asked if I enjoyed teaching her and I realized that I did. I've always liked training, and I think that's the direction I want to go. I was just making a list of things I'm good at that I could possibly make a career out of training people in."

He seemed surprised. "Wow. That's impressive for one day. What do you have so far?"

I rubbed my jaw. "Um self-defense, security, and leadership."

I expected him to laugh at my meager list, but he just nodded. "You should add physical training. You might not want to be a personal trainer, but you are excellent with coming up with the best workout programs and helping the guys with proper form."

That wasn't something that ever crossed my mind. I enjoyed working out and it came naturally to create fitness plans and what exercises to do. I liked helping others get stronger and more confident. I just never would have thought of it as a personal strength.

"Thanks Shane." I wrote it down and was excited to have more to share with Isla. When I first met with my sergeant, the weight of the decisions I needed to make were crushing me. I had no plan, no ideas, just panic. Shane helped, but it was Isla who truly gave me hope. With her assistance, it didn't feel impossible. Now, I had options. I was learning and seeing the different sides of me and suddenly the future wasn't so bleak. There was something to look forward to. A focal point for me to work toward. There might be a lot of unknowns and uncertainty in my life, but now I had a light to guide me.

I couldn't wait for tomorrow to talk with her. As much as I wanted to run to the palace and wake her, I had enough restraint to remain in place. This could wait until morning.

"Shane! Logan! Get up now!" Bill, the head of the security office, burst into our room and continued shouting. "Now! Let's go!"

I rubbed my face as I stepped into my pants. "What's going on?"

Shane was moving quickly, pulling on his boots. "What is it?"

"The princess is missing."

My heart stopped beating.

"What?" I heard Shane yell but it sounded so far away.

"Carolyn went to fetch her this morning. Her bed was empty, but obviously slept in. The grounds are being searched, but an initial check of the palace came up empty. Kyle said he didn't hear anything, and no one came down her hall."

"Logan. Let's go." Shane shook my shoulder and it was enough to break through the cold ice that took over my body. I finished dressing and jogged behind them toward the palace. There were dozens of guards headed in every direction. We went straight to the security office where the king and queen were waiting, watching the wall of screens.

Kyle, Isla's night guard, was pale, standing in the corner. I wanted to slam him against the wall and demand to know how he let this happen, but I knew that wouldn't get me the results I wanted.

I went to the screens and watched her windows. If Kyle didn't see anyone come down her hall, then they had to have used the windows. Her suite had no hidden tunnels or connections to other parts of the palace.

Whoever did this risked being seen, but they hadn't been. How?

"Have you gone through the entire night?" I asked Bill as he took over controls from the man at the computer.

"We have, but there's nothing. It doesn't make sense."

"You've checked the hallway as well?"

"Yes, Kyle never left. He never fell asleep. He didn't miss anything."

I knew what he was trying to convey to me. I couldn't blame Kyle. He did his job correctly. He had no reason to suspect anything was wrong. If someone was able to get into her room, I knew they would be able to get to her without making noise. Nothing would have alerted Kyle that he needed to check.

We didn't have cameras inside Isla's suite for her privacy, which meant we had no idea what happened. There had to be something we missed. The sun rose on the screens and I knew we were already past the time she was taken.

I didn't say it aloud, but I knew that's what happened. Isla didn't leave on her own accord. Not after yesterday. There wasn't a single doubt in my mind. She was removed by force and not by someone who cared about her. Whoever did this was after something else.

"Go back to last night and let's watch again." Bill followed my instructions, but I didn't catch anything the second or third time.

The queen gasped. "Where's my baby. Where's Isla?"

She fell against her husband who didn't take his eyes off the screen. The distraction only took my focus away for a second, but when I looked back to the screen, I caught a flicker.

"Wait!"

Bill paused the feed.

"Go back, slow it down."

We watched in silence as frame by frame, the feed reversed. There it was again. "There. Did you see that?"

Bill nodded. "They took over the feed. They put up another image."

I didn't want to waste time finding it, but I knew if we continued watching, we'd see the second flicker when the feed went live again. "Someone got into the system."

From all I knew about our security that should be impossible.

"How?" King Leo's voice roared.

I looked to Bill, his face pale. This was his team, his room, his domain. If something happened, it had to have been under his watch. One of his men slipped. Or had betrayed them.

My biggest concern was finding Isla before it was too late. "We can worry about that later. Right now, we need to come up with a suspect list and find the princess." I spun to face Shane. "Get the status on every suitor who has come to the palace. Marius left yesterday, but Philippe and Peter should still be here. We can question them, and the rest need to be accounted for."

He nodded and hurried to a different computer, lifting his phone to his ear.

"You think one of them took my daughter?" the queen asked me.

My gut said it was Marius, but that was a serious accusation. One I shouldn't throw out lightly. I took in her despair, her anguish and forgot about what was proper and if it was my place or not.

"I believe it was Marius of Suruso."

The king straightened. "And why would you instantly think of him?"

"He was aggressive toward the princess, possessive and controlling. He didn't respect her boundaries, and I noticed him watching her in a manner none of the other suitors did. He seemed a bit obsessed. He wasn't pleased when she told him to leave yesterday. From the first time I saw him, I had a bad feeling about him."

Queen Anne nodded. "If you think it's him, please do everything you need to get her back."

"Yes, Your Majesty. I will put together a team of my most trusted men. Once I have more information on Marius and his properties, we will leave." I turned my attention to the king. "Sir, if you would reach out to the king and find out what you can, that would be helpful. We need to know if this was done with the crown's assistance."

He understood what I left unsaid. This could be the beginning of a war.

"I will call him now." He turned and left the room while the queen sat next to Bill.

"What time did the switch occur?" she asked.

Bill clicked a few times. "Seven after one this morning."

"It's been almost eight hours. She could be halfway around the world by now." Her voice quivered. I wanted to comfort her, but honestly, a small piece of me blamed her and the king for this. If they had just listened to her and respected her wishes, Marius never would have been here in the first place. Strangers wouldn't have been invited into their home. She never would have been made a target.

But that was cruel right now. She was a mother with a missing child. "Don't worry, Your Majesty. I will find her."

Her eyes found mine, and I saw a flicker of awareness but it was gone as quickly as it came. I didn't have time to figure out what it meant. I had work to do.

I moved to where Shane was working and bent down. "We're going after Marius."

He nodded. "I've already pulled his information. He lives on a vineyard in the south eastern portion of the country. It's secluded but has very little in the way of security."

"Great. I need you to call the guys. Tell them to be ready to leave in an hour."

"Done."

I pulled out my phone and called my sergeant. He would be able to get the equipment and transportation we needed together in time without dealing with red tape.

"McCready, I wasn't expecting to hear from you so soon. Have you made a decision?"

"Not quite, sir. I'm calling about something else." I looked around the room and made sure no one was paying attention to me. "Princess Isla has been taken. We have a suspect and his primary residence. We're putting together a team to go to Suruso now, but I need—"

"Tactical gear and a plane. Understood. I will have everything at the base ready within the hour."

His calm, no nonsense attitude put me at ease. This was a mission and he knew exactly what to do. I did, too. I just needed to focus. I'd led rescues before. I could do this.

"Thank you, sir. I will see you soon."

I slipped my phone back in my pocket and went in search of the king. I needed to know what we were up against before we were in the air.

15

ISLA

This wasn't my bed. I forced my eyes open, fighting through the gritty, dry feeling behind my eyelids and took in my surroundings. This wasn't my room. I sat up and nearly threw up. My head pounded and my stomach rolled. What happened?

I didn't recognize anything around me. The room had soft green walls with tan tile floors. The bed was large with a white and tan duvet. There was a window to my left, but it felt a mile away.

This wasn't the palace. I knew that from the moment I awoke. I could sense it. This room had a Mediterranean vibe. The walls had curved corners, and I could see a red roof outside the building. I stood slowly and took careful, quiet steps toward the window. I leaned against the wall and used it to hold me up and finally reached my goal.

"What?" I gasped. I was surrounded by land in every direction. I'd never seen this landscape before. There were perfectly straight rows of small trees for miles. A vineyard?

My training kicked in. I was safe for the moment. I was being kept in what looked like a mansion not a cement bunker. Whoever had taken me wanted to keep me alive. They also came from money. Either this was some sort of organized crime group, or... my thoughts changed direction and I froze. It was one of the suitors. My gut knew this was right immediately. Any of the men would have this kind of wealth, plus the connections and resources to kidnap a princess.

I had to find a phone. I scanned the room, but it was sparsely decorated with just a bed, chaise, and wardrobe. There was one door directly across from the bed, and one to the right, across from the window. I assumed that was the bathroom, but investigated.

The large ensuite was annoyingly beautiful. Tastefully decorated in tans, pale greens, and blues, it featured a waterfall shower and large soaking tub with a view of the land.

I went to the last door, and turned the knob but it was locked from the outside. Of course. I was on the third floor, so there was a small chance I could jump and land uninjured, but I had no idea where I was. Which direction should I head in? What if I was a hundred kilometers from the nearest neighbor or town? I couldn't be rash. I had to gather more information and make the smart decision.

I didn't hear any voices from the other side of the door, but I tried calling out anyway. "Hello? Is anyone there? Hello!"

I waited and listened for a response but there was nothing. Just silence. Was there even a staff here, or was it just me and my captor? I blew out a breath and moved to sit on the chaise in the far corner. I was going to figure this out. I was smart and resourceful. I'd been trained for this exact situation. I needed to remain calm, focused, and control my impulses. For now, I was safe. I had to stay that way for as long as possible to give my parents time to find me.

Logan.

His face flashed in my mind. He would come for me. He was the very best at what he did. He would already have a plan put together by now. Shane would be helping him. They would guess it was one of the suitors. It was too obvious for them to miss. But which one? Henri, the drunken count who ran at the sight of my brother? Jean, the older man who was more interested in my parents than me? Philippe, hurt that I ditched him during our ride and hadn't bothered to apologize. Or Marius? My skin prickled at the thought of that man. He was forceful and entitled and made me uncomfortable from the moment I laid eyes on him.

My instinct said it was him. Didn't he own a vineyard?

I racked my memory for the details I'd ignored when Carolyn ran through them before each man's arrival. I was pretty sure he was the one. So, he hadn't agreed with my request for him to leave.

He was the most likely man of the lot, and I knew Logan would figure that out. I just had to make sure I gave him time to find me, before Marius… did what? What was his plan with me? I shivered in fear, but forced myself to remember my training. Panicking wouldn't help.

But what to do until Logan came? There wasn't anything in the room to occupy myself. I could take a bath, but the idea of being naked and vulnerable in my captor's home kept me from even considering it.

Being left alone with my thoughts was dangerous.

I could plan more for the Independence Day parade. I already invited the young singer to be my guest and she'd accepted. The only remaining details were a matter of my outfit and making sure the Tarramore palace was prepped for the influx of guests. It was twice the size of the palace I called home, so I wasn't concerned about everyone fitting, but the staff needed to have an accurate count of who was coming.

Serena and Cian's wedding was coming up as well, but they had a team of planners and a small army working to put everything together. My only task was picking out my dress, and I already had an idea I was going to share with Silvia.

Huh. I tapped my thumbs on my thighs. The North Country children's hospital was nearly finished, and I'd attend with Charlie and Aiden in two months for the official ceremony. The next hospital location had been decided, and I received an update last week that work had begun.

I was pretty caught up on everything. Carolyn would be so proud of me. Kidnapped and alone and what was I doing? Running through my responsibilities and making to-do lists.

I knew I should be more afraid, and there was a large part of me that was, but I knew I couldn't succumb to the fear. I had to stay brave and keep a clear head. I had to remain alert and collect as many details as I could. If that meant working while a hostage, then it was what I needed to do.

My training had taught me how to fight if it came to that, but for now I needed to remain calm and cooperate with my captor.

I wondered what my parents were thinking. Did they know who had taken me by now? How were they feeling? I wanted to rub it in their faces that it was their fault I was in this position, but I knew that wasn't really the case. They couldn't have known one of the men was insane. Deep, deep down I knew they were doing what they thought was best for me. Hopefully, now they would back off and let me do things my way.

Surely, this was enough to get them to see my side. If not, maybe it would be better if I stayed here. Ah my first thought of Stockholm syndrome. It was already starting. I was thinking it would be better to be captive than return home. Soon I'd fall for the beast and start talking to the furniture as if they were people.

I couldn't wait to tell Logan how quickly I'd succumbed to the insanity. I was also going to tell him that I no longer accepted his excuses. If he felt about me how I felt about him, as I suspected he did, then there was no reason to keep pushing each other away. I wouldn't let it continue. I knew I loved him. I wanted a future with him. My heart told me he wanted that too. I was done with letting outside forces dictate my life. I would give up my title, my crown, my life of privilege for the chance to be with him forever. If that's what he needed, I would do it in a second without a single regret. He didn't think he could be with me because he wasn't a noble, but it didn't matter to me. I just met some of the most eligible men in Europe and hated every single moment of it. I knew who I wanted to be with. I knew who made me happy. I was ready to fight for us. I'd go against my parents. I'd take on anyone who said we couldn't be together.

It took an extreme event, like getting kidnapped, to make me realize what was worth fighting for. I was done letting anyone else make decisions for me. My parents would understand eventually, and if they didn't, it was their loss. Cian, Aiden, and Ronan would support me. They knew what it was like in my position. How hard it was to trust and to know when someone was being genuine. Heck, it was why Aiden had kept his identity from Charlie when they first met. It was nearly impossible to meet someone who didn't already have a preconceived notion of who we were and how we should behave.

Logan never treated me like that. He got to know me as Isla, not the princess. He asked me questions and spoke to me like an equal. We formed a friendship that turned into real feelings.

I loved him. I knew it, and I was ready to tell him. If he had the strength to walk away from me after I admitted that to him, then I had to let him go and respect his decision. But

I didn't think he would. I think he needed me to make the first move, test the waters and prove to him it was safe. I could do that for him. I wanted to. It was one of the rare times I could be the one to protect him.

There was a knock on the door before I heard it unlock and open quietly. A girl, close to my age, walked in carrying a silver tray. The moment her eyes found me she froze and her mouth opened.

"Hello?" I stood and waited for her to approach me. She seemed terrified, and I didn't want to scare her away.

Her eyes dropped and she marched forward to set the tray on the end of the chaise. She bowed and kept her eyes on the ground.

"Thank you."

Her shoulders sagged and she peered up at me for a split second.

"What's your name?"

"Ana." The word was barely a whisper.

"Ana, can you tell me where I am?"

She sank further into herself, and I worried she would collapse. "I'm so sorry, Your Highness."

"You know who I am?" I wasn't completely shocked, I was fairly recognizable but her behavior confused me.

She nodded and took in a shuddered breath. "My master said he had a guest in this room who needed breakfast. He said you were unwell and that's why we needed to keep your door locked."

Her gaze lifted to meet my own. "I heard that he brought an unconscious woman home last night, but none of us knew it was you. I'm so sorry, Your Highness."

"Please, Ana, call me Isla." I wanted to reach out to her, but she was so skittish I didn't want her to run away. "Is your master Lord Marius?"

She nodded.

"Ana, I didn't come here willingly. He drugged me and took me from my home in Lochland. I'm not sure what he has planned for me, but I need to let my family know where I am."

Her eyes darted around the room. "I promise, Ms. Isla. None of us knew."

"And none of you will be punished. We will help you all leave. If you need new jobs or housing, we will take care of you."

Something in my words lit a fire in her eyes. "Really, Miss?"

"Yes, I promise. Everyone here, with the exception of Marius and any of his accomplices, will be helped."

A new strength seemed to fill her. "My family has worked here for three generations. His family has kept us as slaves. He provides only the most basic necessities. If you can help us…"

"I promise, Ana. I will get you and your family away from him."

She nodded. "I will be back. I will find a way for you to contact your family."

"Thank you." I threw my arms around her and hugged her thin shoulders. She tensed, and I took a step back.

"I'll be back, Ms. Isla." She turned and walked out of the room, and I heard the lock click back in place. I was putting my trust in a terrified young woman. Hopefully she believed me enough to help.

16

LOGAN

I stared across the bare plane to where Shane was giving the team updates and sharing what information we already had on Marius. I hadn't been in a military plane in over two years, and after traveling around with Isla in the royal jet, it was a shock to be back. It helped me get in the right headspace, though. I was reminded that this wasn't a vacation or diplomatic trip. This was a rescue mission, the most important one I'd ever done.

The king seemed to have aged ten years in the time it took us to get prepared this morning. After he spoke to the Suruso's king and learned that Lord Marius had been dismissed from the court the year before and had spent his entire family multimillion-euro fortune, he knew we had our suspect. I wasn't sure yet how this information didn't come up in our research, but from past experience I assumed he paid someone to bury it. Their king had no idea Marius had come to Lochland and was appalled to learn that he was behind the kidnapping of our princess. Their military was heading to Marius's remote vineyard, and we were assured we'd have their complete corporation. They didn't want this to escalate into anything more than it already had.

King Leo was ready to declare war and call in the rest of the European Royals to back him, but luckily the queen was able to rein him in. We didn't want to do anything to spook Marius and force him to make an impulsive decision.

"Logan," Shane called out and when he had my attention, he continued. "Cian received a call from Isla. She is at Marius's vineyard. She's safe and Cian told her we're on our way."

Relief like I never knew was possible washed over me. She was okay. She was safe. She was exactly where we thought she was. The worst thing that could have happened was us wasting time flying to Suruso only to find they were in Columbia or somewhere else on the other side of the world.

"That's great news. Has their military arrived yet?"

He shook his head. "Not yet."

I was about to ask another question when he held up his hand, signaling that he was listening to the communication device in his ear. His eyebrows rose and he shook his head. "The palace just received a ransom request. Marius wants twenty million in exchange for the princess."

"What?" My voice roared over the sound of the engines. All of the men looked up at me with concern. "He's insane."

Shane agreed. "The king is attempting to establish contact. They hope to distract him so the military can get in place, and we can get there."

At least we knew that Marius had every intention of keeping her alive and unharmed for now. Did he really think this would work? That the king of Lochland could be bullied? That his daughter could be used as a pawn? He chose the wrong country to mess with, especially now that we had his own king on our side. There was no way this would end well for the lord. He'd be tried in both countries, although I doubted Isla would want him to remain in her country. He'd serve out his sentence with the people who turned their backs on him.

"Twenty minutes. The pilot says there's an area he can land in close to the vineyard. Our transportation will meet us there."

I was more than ready to get moving and feel like I was actually doing something. I just needed Isla back where she belonged. Safe and with me. It had only been twelve hours since she was taken, but it felt like eternity had passed since Bill woke us up this morning.

"Everyone ready?" I waited for each member of our ten-man team to confirm. We were each armed, but I didn't expect us to have to use force. The moment Marius realized he was surrounded, he'd be a fool not to surrender. My only hope was that he didn't do anything crazy and use Isla as a tool or shield to protect himself.

I wouldn't let that happen. The first thing I wanted was to establish a visual of Isla. Once I knew she was safe and away from Marius, we would go in. Anyone who posed a threat to the princess would be eliminated. I had no flexibility on that.

Time seemed to move in fast-forward from the time we touched down. A Suruso soldier, Alec, met me at the door and instantly filled me in with their progress.

"Our teams have established a perimeter around the residence and the house. We looked through records and didn't see any tunnels or other means of getting away other than the main road that leads to the nearest town. There are two cars registered to Marius and we have confirmed that both at the house. A tighter perimeter has been made closer to the house, and we're waiting on your order to move in."

We climbed into a waiting black truck and Shane and two

others joined us while the rest loaded into the second vehicle.

"Have you confirmed the princess's location?"

"Yes, sir. She is in a room on the third floor."

"Maintain a visual of her at all times."

"Yes, sir." He picked up a phone and spoke into it in a language I didn't understand.

"How many should we expect?"

"We've only seen staff, no armed men."

What was Marius' plan? "How far away are we?"

"Less than five minutes."

The winding road followed the rolling hills that spread in every direction. The countryside was beautiful, but I didn't have time or mental space to appreciate it. I focused on the path in front of us and waited to spot the house.

"There." The driver pointed at a white mansion sitting in a valley surrounded by impeccable rows of trees. What a beautiful place for such an ugly person.

I spotted the first line of soldiers and the building nerves kicked into full-force adrenaline. I was ready for this.

"Tell your men to shoot on sight if anyone approaches the princess." Alec didn't hesitate before passing along my message. Once we were closer, the driver stopped and I jumped out with Shane at my side.

"What's your plan?"

"We're going to knock on the door."

He laughed. "Wait, really?"

"How else do we let him know we're here?"

He paused, falling behind.

"I'm not going to ask for a cup of tea, Shane. I'm going to get him out of the house, detain him, then go get the princess."

He huffed but caught up and shook his head. "Yes, sir."

I approached the small front gate and kicked it open. The

wide double doors of the house swung open and an elderly man looked at us with a terrified expression. I rested my rifle to my side and tried to appear somewhat less threatening.

"Where is Lord Marius?"

He blinked and spun around, leaving the doors open. His shuffle seemed to be as fast as he could walk but at this rate, we might find our man tomorrow. I moved forward and followed the man.

"What are you doing? We want him to come out, not us go in. We don't have coverage inside."

I paused at the threshold and held my gun up. He was right. We were vulnerable inside, but that didn't mean I was going to greet the vile man with a smile.

Voices shouted from deep inside the house and within thirty seconds, Marius rounded a corner with a stunned expression. His eyes found my face, then my gun, and he stopped mid-step.

"What are *you* doing here?"

"Getting our princess." I pointed the gun at him. "Why don't you come outside for a few minutes. I believe there are some people who wish to speak to you."

His eyes widened and I heard the footsteps of the soldiers behind me.

"No. No. This isn't right."

I narrowed my eyes. "Time to come out."

He shook his head. "No, she's mine. I need her."

The soldiers were taking slow steps to surround him, and his primitive survival instincts seemed to kick in. He raised his arms, ready to defend himself. "She's mine."

"No, Lord Marius." Alec spoke to him in their native tongue and I watched Marius become more deranged. They were yelling back and forth and finally Marius crumbled to the ground on his knees. He was weeping, and Alec shot forward, tying his hands behind his back before binding his ankles together.

Shane glanced at me. "Let's get our princess."

A young woman stepped out from a hallway and waved to us. "Please, she's this way."

We followed after her and she took us to a back staircase and up to the top floor. She hurried to the last door and pulled a key out of her pocket. Once she unlocked and opened the door, she waved us forward.

I entered the room and nearly cried when I saw Isla standing, looking out the window. She turned and stared at me, her own tears falling down her cheeks. I rushed forward and pulled her into my arms.

"Logan?"

"I've got you. You're safe."

She broke, falling against my chest and weeping.

"You did so good. You were so brave." I continued whispering reassurances to her. "Did he hurt you?"

She shook her head. "No, I never even saw him."

I was relieved, but that didn't mean he didn't hurt her sense of peace and security. This was likely to have lasting effects, but I would be with her to work through it. I was never leaving her again.

Holding her, I had a realization that nearly made me fall to the floor.

I wasn't going to ever let anything take her from me again.

This was it. I wanted her, I loved her, and I was ready to fight for her. I knew the odds were stacked against me and I had more than a few things to prove, but I wasn't going to give up. I wouldn't ever let her walk away again. I was done pushing her away. I would never turn her down again. If it meant leaving the service, if it meant giving up the only life I'd ever known, it would be worth it. I loved this woman with my whole heart. I couldn't continue to pretend she was anything less than my entire world. She wasn't just the princess or just the person I was assigned to protect. She was everything.

"Isla." She tilted her head up to meet my eyes. "I'm so sorry. I'm sorry I wasn't there. That I couldn't protect you."

"Oh Logan, it's not your fault. I don't remember anything, so I don't know how he did it, but he was obviously careful and planned this out."

Shane cleared his throat and I remembered we weren't alone.

"I'm glad you're okay, Isla."

"Thanks Shane." She smiled at him, then turned to the girl that let us in. "I'll eternally be grateful for all you did for me, Ana. I will keep my promise."

I looked at the other woman. She seemed to tremble under all the attention. "You kept Isla safe?"

She nodded.

"You have the thanks of the king and queen of Lochland. We are all in your debt."

Her eyes widened and she began to protest but Isla held up her hand. "My brother is on his way here. He's the future king and will be able to make all the arrangements for you and your family. If you know where you would like to go, he will make it happen. If you and your family need a place to live, we will set that up. Whatever you need, I will make sure you and your family are taken care of."

She sounded like a true princess in that moment.

"Marius has been detained," Shane cut in. "When you're ready, we will leave."

Isla looked around the room. "I want to leave, but I'm not going back to the palace."

I narrowed my eyes. "What do you mean?"

She sighed. "I need time to process everything that's

happened in the past few weeks. I need time to be alone and figure out what I want."

The word *alone* felt like a knife to my chest. "Right. Of course."

"I want you to come with me, Logan. Let Shane handle things here. Let my parents and brothers worry about the rest. Please, just come with me."

I didn't need to be asked twice. "Of course, I will."

She smiled and tightened her arms around me. "I want to go to my house. Can you get us there?"

I'd never actually been to Isla's private residence on the coast, but I knew where it was and how to get there. "Yes. Just give me a moment."

Shane was already getting information from Ana. He didn't need to be told what to do, but the smile he shot toward me told me he'd heard enough to know what was going on. He knew I'd made my decision.

I entered the hall and pulled out my phone. I called Aiden and waited for him to answer.

"Do you have her?" He didn't bother with a greeting.

"Yes, she's safe. He didn't hurt her."

He sighed. "Thank you. Now bring her home."

"I can't do that."

"What do you mean?" His voice sounded impatient.

"She isn't ready to come back yet. She needs some time to process, and I'm not going to force her to do anything she doesn't want to."

There was a pause before he sighed again. "You're right. Where does she want to go?"

"Her house."

"Of course."

"Can you get us there?"

"Yes, I'll have a plane waiting for you guys. I'll call and get the house ready as well. I'll send you a message with the rest of the details."

"Thank you."

"No, Logan. Thank you. Now, take care of my sister. She needs you." That wasn't what I was expecting, what did he mean she needs me?

Before I could ask, he hung up and I went back to Isla. "It's all set."

"Thank you." She hugged Ana and Shane before walking toward me. I led her down the stairs and outside, away from the activity at the front of the house. My phone vibrated in my pocket and I pulled it out to see a message from Aiden with a location. That's where the plane would be.

I found Alec and called to him. His eyes locked on Isla and his face paled. He hurried over and bowed. "Your Highness, words cannot express my remorse."

She waved him off. "I appreciate it, but I don't hold anyone responsible except Marius. I don't think ill of Suruso or it's people."

That seemed to make him feel much better. "Your grace and mercy will be made known, Your Highness."

"Alec, I appreciate all you've done to help, but I need one more favor. We need a ride."

He called over his shoulder to a tall man waiting near a black SUV. "Of course. Alex will take you wherever you need. We will take care of the rest of your men as well."

"Thank you, Alec."

I led Isla to the waiting vehicle and the moment we pulled away from the house, she seemed to relax. Her hand found mine, and she slipped her fingers between mine. For the first time ever, I didn't care if anyone saw.

17

ISLA

Seven. That was the number of people we'd met so far and the number of people who witnessed Logan holding my hand without a care in the world. Did he realize he was doing it or was his mind distracted from the events of the day? Either way, I wasn't going to point it out. Having him touch me in public was new and exciting, but it also felt right. He had a way of making me feel safe and protected, but more importantly, valued. Like I was something to be cherished. He felt like my equal.

So many men had tried to control me or claim me or twist me into what they thought I should be. They wanted me to be a pretty trophy to stand by their side, to be seen but not heard.

Logan was the first man to ask me for my opinion and listen to it. He made me feel like I mattered. It was ironic that he made me feel like we were on even ground when he thought that was the biggest obstacle in our way. He worried my title made me out of his reach, but he was so very wrong. I was going to find a way to explain this to him. It was time to lay it all out and hold nothing back.

A driver I didn't recognize was waiting for us when we landed. He simply smiled and drove us the short distance to my home. The cottage was located on the western coast, overlooking hundreds of foot cliffs. My grandfather had gifted it to me so I'd always have a place of my own. Aiden and Rowan each received larger manors, but I loved my modest home. It had been my grandparents' favorite place to escape, and I appreciated the appeal in a way my brothers never did.

The second I saw the white-washed fence, my entire body relaxed for the first time in weeks. The grey building with the sloped roof called to me.

"It's stunning," Logan whispered as he leaned forward to see out the window. My heart swelled at his reaction. I wanted him to love this place as much as I did. I wanted it to be our home. A place we could come to escape the world and find peace.

The driver parked in front and I opened my door and hurried out before he had a chance to move. Logan followed after me, chuckling. "A bit excited?"

"You have no idea. It's been months since I've had a chance to visit." I pushed open the front door and beamed. Someone had come through and opened the windows so the salty ocean air filled the space.

Logan stepped up next to me. "It's bigger than it looks from the outside."

"Five bedrooms, four baths, but most importantly, this." I took his hand and led him through the main hall to the other end. The entire back porch was made of glass windows that could slide open and gave view to the cliffs. I've spent countless hours sitting out here. It's where I do my best thinking and daydreaming.

"This is stunning. I had no idea." Logan leaned against the window and looked out. "Can we stay here forever?"

I slid next to him and rested my head against his arm. "Yes, please."

"I can see why you wanted to come here. It's so peaceful."

"It's the only place that is purely my own. It doesn't belong to the crown or my family. It's all mine."

"Really?"

"Yeah, it was my grandparents' vacation home. Before they passed, they gave Aiden, Rowan, and me a property. Aiden's manor is near the palace in Ballivaughn and Rowan's is in Scotland. Neither of them understood why I was so excited to get this home rather than their large estates, but they never loved this place like I did. My grandparents brought us here once a year while we were growing up. It was the only place I felt like I could be myself. I was just a child, not a princess. They didn't care if I played in the mud or came to the dinner table covered in dirt. I was free here."

He turned to face me and took my hands in his. "Thank you for sharing it with me."

I smiled. "You're the only person outside our family I've ever brought here. I usually come alone, or with Carolyn."

He smirked. "She's not family."

"Maybe not technically, but I think of her as an older, wiser sister."

"I'm honored." He stared into my eyes, and I felt something shift. This was the first time we'd ever been truly alone. After everything that happened in the past twenty-four hours, he was the only one I wanted to be with. He made me feel safe. When I woke up in a strange place, alone and confused, I knew he was coming for me. I never felt too afraid because I knew it was only a matter of time. When I was able to call Cian, he assured me Logan was on his way. I just had to be strong until he arrived.

"Logan, I don't know how to thank you."

"You don't need to thank me for doing my job."

Ugh. That word made me cringe. "Is that all it is?"

He frowned. "Isla, you know it's not. I didn't mean it like that. I would have come for you no matter what. The second I found out you were missing, my world stopped spinning. The only thing that mattered was finding you. I'm just so grateful my first instinct was right. We were on the plane headed to Suruso when you called Cian and let him know where you were. I was worried we were heading in the wrong direction, but it was like my heart and soul knew where you were."

"The moment I realized what happened, everything you taught me about staying calm and buying time took over, and I knew you were on your way. I was honestly never that scared because of that."

He leaned forward and kissed my forehead. I closed my eyes, reveling in the contact. I needed him to know. My body couldn't contain it a second longer. I tilted my head up to him and saw emotions swirling in his eyes.

"What's wrong?"

His hesitation made my heart race. A million thoughts ran through my mind and none of them good.

"Isla, I don't want to take advantage of this situation."

"What do you mean?" I searched his face for a sign of what he was trying to tell me.

"You've been through so much, not just today. The past few weeks have been a lot for you. Your parent's decision to invite strangers to come meet you. The disruption to your life. There's been so much and I completely understand that you'd feel overwhelmed or emotional. I want to be here for you, but I also want you to have the space you need to think and sort through everything." He paused and I tried to interrupt but he continued. "I don't want you to jump into anything or make any decisions you may regret later."

I shook my head, not understanding where this was all coming from. "You don't want to be with me?"

All the progress I thought we made felt like it was flying over the edge of the cliffs and crashing into the Atlantic.

"No, I…" He rubbed his hand over his face. "I just don't want to pressure you into anything after all you've been through. I'm trying to give you a chance to process on your own. You said back at the… you said you needed space. I'm trying to give that to you."

"I don't need to process. I know exactly what I want and what will make me happy."

He flinched like I'd punched him. "I want that to be me, more than anything. But Isla, can you honestly say that a life with me is what you pictured for yourself?"

Now it was my turn to feel hurt. "What do you mean, Logan? Did I imagine and dream of falling in love with a good, honest, loving man? Yes. That's exactly what I've always wanted."

He sighed and looked away. "I want it to be that simple, but it's not. Not for us."

"Because I'm a princess?"

"And because I'm a Marine. I'm your guard."

I was getting more and more frustrated. "Stop using that as a wall to hide behind."

"It's the truth. We can't ignore it."

"What does it matter? If you were a baker or an artist or a member of parliament, it wouldn't change anything."

He closed his eyes. "I'm not trying to hurt you or push you away. I just need to know that you really understand how much is at stake. Neither of us can be impulsive or selfish."

So, that's what he thought of me right now? "I understand perfectly." My voice shook with each word. "I think you're right. I do need some space to process."

I turned and hurried to the stairs, heading to the room I'd claimed. I shut the door behind me and collapsed on the bed. How had things gone from perfect to completely wrecked so quickly?

I thought we were on the same page. We were supposed to be enjoying being alone for the first time ever. We should be cuddling on the porch, soaking in the feeling of being in each other's arms.

I let out a frustrated sigh. This wasn't at all what I wanted. I thought coming here would give us a chance to put the politics and expectations aside, just for a few days. Why was it always the same thing? Yes, I had responsibilities and there were plenty of eyes watching me. Each person thought they knew best for my life, but when was the last time someone asked me directly?

I just wanted to shut out the world and be with Logan, let him see what being together would be like. I knew in my heart we were meant to be together. I knew my feelings weren't one sided. I was scared, too. I just didn't let that overshadow everything else.

He had pressure on him too. So why didn't he see that as something we had in common, something that only we could truly understand about each other rather than a reason to keep us apart?

Now would be a wonderful time to have Charlie or Serena around to talk to, but I wasn't ready for the world to know my location. They knew I was safe and with Logan, and for now that had to be enough.

He was right. I did need space to process everything, but not my feelings for him. Not wanting to be together.

18

LOGAN

I messed up. The second she walked away, I should have gone after her, but I believed what I told her. Things had been crazy and following that up with us flying off to be alone was just the tip of the iceberg.

Making her mad was the last thing I wanted, but I wouldn't take advantage of her vulnerability. Wasn't that a sign of how much I truly cared? I was trying to be selfless and put her needs first. If that made me the enemy right now, I'd accept that.

It was still my duty to protect her, even from herself. Plus, there were worse places to be stuck while she decompressed. I hadn't been out to see the cliffs in almost ten years. My few days off were usually spent with my family or resting. Getting out to do sight-seeing hadn't been a priority.

The cliffs were a reminder of how small I was in the grand scheme of things. They were the end of our country. The breakoff that formed our border. They were magnificent. I wanted to enjoy them, but I couldn't. Not while Isla was mad at me.

I turned my back to the view and sent a text to Aiden and Cian letting them know we arrived safely, then called Shane.

"Hi, Logan." His voice sounded tired.

"Everything sorted?"

"Yes, he's been taken into custody. The king agreed to him being prosecuted for all of his crimes in Suruso. He doesn't want him to ever return to Lochland."

"Isla will be happy to hear that."

"How is she?" The concern in his voice made me feel guilty for not keeping him updated during our travels. He cared about her too, and her safety mattered to him as much as it did to me.

"There's a lot to work through, but she'll be okay."

"I know. She's a tough one."

I chuckled. That was putting it lightly. "I'll let you know when we're planning on coming back to the palace."

"Don't rush, Logan."

"What's that supposed to mean?" I knew he was teasing.

"This is a better opportunity than you could have dreamed of. Don't waste it."

"Understood."

"Good. Take care of her."

"I will."

After ending the call, I wandered back through the house, giving myself a tour. To an outsider, they would be shocked Isla called this home. It was a modest size and had an amazing view, but it wasn't what anyone would picture for a royal. There were no stately gardens or high walls. It was unassuming and cozy.

The decorations were simply done in white, grey, and navy. It was tasteful and not too dated. I wondered if she had it redone since her grandparents passed, or if this was their choosing. Even though it wasn't lavish or impressive, it was perfect for Isla. It embodied her warmth, gentleness, and appreciation for what others often overlook.

I found the kitchen and was pleased it had been stocked before our arrival. The staff only had a few hours' notice, and they'd outdone themselves. I removed all the items needed for corned beef sandwiches and began making two. If there was one thing I'd learned over the last two years, it was that a hungry Isla was a much harder person to get to listen to reason. She was often grumpy and impatient until being fed. If I wanted her to forgive me quickly, it was best to come with an offering. I just hoped she'd had enough time to fume and was ready to talk again.

Since I didn't find her in my perusal of the first floor, I took both plates and some bottles of water before heading upstairs. There was a long hall of doors, but only one was shut so I headed toward it. I knocked and waited for her to allow me in. The motion took me back to the palace. No matter how far we were, I was reminded of who I was even in the smallest details.

"Come in, Logan."

I sighed and opened the door. She rolled to her side to face me on the bed with her arm bent to hold up her head. I was expecting a shoe to be thrown at me but she seemed calm.

"I brought you food." I held out the offering hoping to win her over.

She eyes the plate. "What is it?"

"Corned beef."

"With mustard?"

"Of course."

"No sauerkraut?"

"Never."

A smile cracked her lips. "Thank you."

She swung her legs around so she was sitting up and held out her hands. I gave her the plate and sat next to her.

"I'm sorry." There was more I needed to say, but that was the most important.

She ignored me, taking a bite and moaning. "This is exactly what I needed."

I tried not to take that too personally. Hungry Isla didn't always think things through.

"I know better than to tell you what you need. You get enough of that from everyone else. The last person who should be adding to that is me."

She took another bite, not speaking.

"That wasn't what I was trying to do though. I simply wanted to make sure you had time for yourself. We're here so you can be alone and unbothered. I didn't want to add to your stress."

She swallowed and demurely dabbed at her mouth with a napkin I'd brought up. "I understand. I did say I needed space, but I didn't mean from you."

I sucked in a breath. That was not what I was expecting.

"There is so much of my life that's controlled by others. My day to day life is handled by someone else. My time is scheduled based on other people's needs. I'm told what to do, where to go, sometimes even what to say. I understand that it's a part of my role, but I need a place where those rules don't apply. A sanctuary where I can be completely myself." She ducked her head and picked at the bread. "I feel that with you."

"Isla–"

"Don't start in with the excuses, Logan. I have them all memorized. I've tried to show you that there's more to life, more to you, than just your job. You have other passions and skills. You can have a future without the Marines if that's what you want. If you want to stay, that's fine too. All I've ever wanted was for you to see your own potential and take control. You have that ability. I don't."

"I appreciate that, Isla. You've shown me there's more to life than following orders. I'm scared of what comes next, though."

Her eyes held mine. "What's that?"

"I don't know. It's not just for me to decide," I whispered. This was the closest I'd ever come to admitting my feelings. To telling her that I wanted her in my future.

"You're speaking in code."

I held her eyes. "I can't make any decisions without all the information."

"What do you need to know?"

This was it. It was time for me to lay it all out for her. No one was going to barge in. No maids or assistants or guards. No interruptions. No emergencies to distract us. Just me and her.

"I can't make any permanent decisions about my future and my career without knowing what you want."

Her eyebrows pulled together. "What I want?"

My stomach rolled at the thought of having to spell this out, but there couldn't be any room for misunderstanding. Not right now.

"I need to know how you feel about me. What future you want for yourself and if it involves me. Did you mean what you said downstairs?"

She made no move. Just stared at me until what felt like hours had passed, and she smiled. "You're going to let me say it this time?"

I nodded. "I don't want you to hold back."

"I want you, Logan. You can try to give me all the space and time in the world, but I don't need to think about it. I know exactly how I feel about you."

"But it isn't just that, Isla. It's not that simple. You might have feelings for me, but please try to think past this moment. Past staying at this house. Think about telling your parents, the public, the government. Are you ready for that ridicule? The hate we'll receive? Not just from the people in Lochland, but from around the world. They don't want to see two people like us together. They want their romantic fairy tales. You're the country's sweetheart. The people want you to marry someone famous. They hold you to the highest standard."

She waited for me to finish, then smiled. "Logan, I know all of that. I've faced it my entire life. You don't think I heard backlash when I chose my university? When I decided to focus on children's charities? Every single decision I've made has come with unwelcome feedback. I know there will be pressure and questions and opinions, but none of that matters to me. I choose you."

I needed to hear that, more than she could know, but there was still a part of me that held back from fully accepting it.

"We'll need your parents' blessing. That's not an option."

She sighed. "I know. It might take time, but they'll come around. Once they see how happy we make each other."

That's where the majority of my doubt laid. I didn't think the king and queen would care about our feelings. They would look at me, my upbringing, my job, my station, and turn me away. They'd probably have me assigned as far away from her as possible.

"You have to believe me, Logan. I know them. All they really want is for me to be happy. They might go about it the wrong way at times, but they won't refuse me."

"I can't provide a life you're used to. I have some money saved, but it's not much compared to—"

"Don't compare yourself to anyone else. You've worked incredibly hard for Lochland, my family, and me. Don't diminish that." She sighed. "Look around you, this is my favorite place in the world. Not a five-star hotel in the French Riviera. Not a villa in Tuscany or an island in the Caribbean. My cottage is my happiest place. With you here, I have all I could ever want."

I smiled and looked around the room. There was the bed we were on, two nightstands, and a chair near the window. That was all. It was less than half the size of her room at the palace, but she was right. It was all we could ever need or want.

"I can't buy you jewels."

"I prefer chocolates." She winked.

"No fancy cars or thoroughbred horses."

"I'd settle for a dog."

I chuckled. "Your closet won't always be packed with the newest designs off the runway."

"You know I prefer comfy sweats whenever possible."

She was going to have a retort for everything I tried. It made me fall for her even more.

"Isla, you deserve the world. I can't live knowing I'm responsible for not providing you with it."

She leaned forward until she was mere inches away. "All I could ever want is in this room right now."

I opened my mouth to argue, but her grin caught me off guard.

"Logan, I love you."

My mouth opened, but nothing came out. Then her words hit me and I couldn't stop myself. "I love you so much, Isla. I have since the moment I met you."

This was all I'd ever wanted.

I lowered my lips to hers, sealing our admissions. My chest felt like it was going to burst open.

I trailed my fingertips along her cheek, behind her neck,

and into her hair. I held her close, perfectly content to stay in this moment forever.

She opened her mouth and sighed against me before sealing her lips to mine once more.

She pulled back just enough to speak. "Please don't run from me."

I rested my forehead against hers. "I won't. I don't think I could at this point. It would kill me."

"Whatever comes next, we can deal with. We can handle it together."

"Okay."

That one word held so much promise. I was ready to fight for us. We were going to have to face her parents and family, but it didn't matter. Together we could do anything.

"I'm going to finish my sandwich now." She pulled back with a silly smile and I chuckled. I picked up my own and devoured it in just a few bites. The last time I ate was the night before. I'd been too stressed to think of anything but getting to Isla to even consider stopping for something as frivolous as eating.

Once we were done, she took my plate with hers and set them on the nightstand. "Okay, let's be serious."

I tried not to smile, but she was sitting cross legged in the middle of a bed, still in her pajamas from the night before, and she wanted to be serious? "Yes, let's."

She pursed her lips and glared at me before starting again. "What are you going to do?"

"As far as my job?"

She nodded.

The choice was obvious. I knew if I ever got the opportunity to be with Isla, that was the sign I'd need to know it was time to leave active duty. "I'll let my sergeant know it's time for me to be discharged."

"You're sure? I don't want you to have any regrets. If you aren't ready to leave, you don't have to. We can wait."

I shook my head. "No, I'm ready. I might not know what I'm going to do with myself, but I'm ready to end this chapter."

"That means not being my guard anymore."

I almost laughed. "It might not be my official title, but I promise I will never stop being your protector."

She smiled and leaned forward, placing a sweet kiss on my lips before pulling back. "I know."

"Good." I grinned.

"Would you accept a room in the palace?"

Her question caught me off guard. I had no idea what to say.

"Serena and Charlie both live there. It's easier for everyone."

I knew it was strategic from a security angle to keep everyone under one roof as much as possible. It made everything much easier to manage rather than dividing resources just so Charlie or Serena could live in an apartment in town. It didn't make sense, not when the palace had plenty of room and they so quickly merged into the princes' lives, accepting roles that supported the crown's philanthropic efforts.

It was an easy decision for them, but for me? I didn't know what to think. Could I go from a guard to a guest? How would the staff feel? Would it cause problems? I wasn't concerned so much about their opinions, but I did respect them. If it made people uncomfortable then I would have to take that into consideration.

"I'm not sure. I didn't think about that. I guess I assumed I'd find my own place."

She cocked an eyebrow. "Do we really need to have this argument? You know I'll win. I have your very own reasoning on my side."

I barked out a laugh. "You're right. The moment we go public with our relationship there will be a target on my back. I have just as much reason to stay in the palace as Charlie or Serena. I might be able to take care of myself, but it wouldn't be fair to the security team. That is, if your parents allow it."

She waved off my concern. "Once we get over the hurdle of them accepting us as a couple, you having a room in the palace will be a given."

That was true. The scariest step was going to be approaching her parents and risking their rejection. I knew they liked me as a guard, and maybe even as a person, but that didn't mean they would be quick to give us their blessing. Isla was able to play it cool and act like this wasn't a huge deal, but I knew their approval was important to her. As her mom and dad, they had a lot of sway and influence over her happiness. As the king and queen, they could forbid our relationship from continuing.

All we could do was hope for the best. It might take time for them to accept the idea of us together, but I wasn't going to give up easily. Not after how long I'd waited for this day.

"We'll survive this, right?" I asked with a laugh, but I really did need some reassurance.

"We will. It would help if we had my brothers on our side first."

The thought of talking to Aiden and Cian, and even Rowan, was almost as daunting as the king and queen. Those guys were friendly with me, but that's because they only saw me as their sister's guard. Once they realized I was interested in her in a less than professional manner, that would probably change.

"When do you want to talk to them?" I asked, hoping it was days or weeks from now.

"I think we should call them tomorrow."

I cringed and she laughed. "Don't let them scare you. You know they like you."

"They might not after this."

She smiled. "They want me to be happy, and you're the one who makes me happy, so they have to like you. Charlie and Serena will help."

She might have been joking about the last part, but it was true. I'd have to get them on my side to help convert her brothers, then use all of them to win over her parents. This was turning into a war strategy.

I laughed. "There's an awful lot of planning and politics involved in this. Who knew I'd be using my training so soon."

She smiled and took my hand. "We'll get through this."

"Is that all we're going to say to each other for the next little while?"

"Yes."

I lifted her hand to my lips and pressed a kiss on her knuckles. "That's all I need."

19

ISLA

I heard voices coming from downstairs the moment I opened my eyes. Logan asked for no staff to be here. We had plenty of food, clothing, and toiletries. There was no reason for anyone to be here.

I swung my legs over the side of the bed and stood. I pulled on my robe and tied it around my waist before heading down to investigate. It didn't take more than a few steps for me to recognize what was going on.

They found me. Well, us.

I took in a soothing breath and prayed for the strength I would need before heading to the kitchen.

"There she is," Cian said with too much enthusiasm.

Aiden held out his arms like he was making a formal announcement. "Sleeping beauty has decided to grace us with her presence."

I rolled my eyes and looked for Logan. He was in front of the stove focused on the two pans. As if ignoring them would make them disappear. Poor guy. I'd tried that for years with no success.

"What are you guys doing here?" I tried to give them an intimidating glare but neither of them seemed to notice.

"Our dear parents are out of their minds with worry. We told them we'd check in on you personally and assure them you are in fact, just fine," Aiden said. Charlie walked in from the other end of the room.

"There you are!" She hurried to me and pulled me into a tight hug. Her displays of affection had taken time to get used to, but now they were comforting. "I'm so glad you're okay."

When she released me, I leaned against the counter. "Me too."

Serena appeared and we repeated the hugging before I escaped to the safety of Logan. He smiled at me and began loading plates with eggs and sausage. "Food's ready. Let's sit and talk."

Everyone followed his orders and soon we were gathered around the country style table. I looked around at the people I loved and couldn't believe it. I never imagined we'd all be together in my home like this, especially not with Logan sitting at the head, across from Cian.

"So, what's going on? Why are we here and not in Ballivaughn?" Aiden asked the question I figured was on everyone's mind.

"Once Logan got to me, I needed to get away. I needed space from everything. I knew people would fawn over me as soon as I got back to the palace. There would be questions and meetings and it was too overwhelming to even think about. Since the moment Dad announced he was inviting suitors into our home I've been a wreck. He took over my schedule. He cancelled meetings that were important to me. He forced me to interact with men I had zero interest in. What little control I had over my life vanished." I looked to Logan and sighed.

"When I saw Logan, I knew I had to take the opportunity to get away before anyone could try to stop me. I didn't want either of you showing up and taking me back to Mum and Dad."

Cian's eyes narrowed. "You really think we would have ignored your wishes and forced you to do something you didn't want? After all you've already been through?"

I shrugged. "Honestly, yes."

Aiden shook his head. "You're our sister, Isla. We love you. Your happiness and well-being is our primary concern. Forget about what our parents say. We have your back, always."

I didn't want this to turn into bashing our parents. Ninety percent of the time they were amazing and did everything they could to ensure our happiness. This was the biggest disagreement we'd ever had.

"Thank you. I appreciate that. It's just … after everything that happened, I needed to feel like I had some control over my life. This was the only place I wanted to be."

"You had a night to yourself. You couldn't really expect us to stay away longer than that." Aiden said with a pained look in his eyes. We'd always been close and he was used to me turning to him. It was time to let him know there was another important man in my life. I tried to put on a brave face, but I wasn't sure how he or Cian were going to take this.

"I'm sure Dad had a pure intent when he started this. I have to believe he thought he was doing what was best for me, and that Mum agreed, but they were wrong. I didn't need anyone coming into my life. I already have a man I love."

Charlie winked at me while everyone else stared at me like I'd grown another head. I turned to Logan and grabbed his hand. "We're in love. We have been for a while, but it's taken a bit of time to get out of our own way."

The room was so silent. I felt like they could all hear my heart racing, it was pounding so loud in my ears.

"Finally." Aiden broke the silence and it was like he popped a balloon.

"I believe you owe me a hundred Euro," Serena told Cian with a sassy smile.

Cian groaned and pulled his wallet out of his back pocket. He pulled out the bill and slapped it into her waiting palm.

Charlie was clapping and smiling wide. "I'm so happy for both of you."

Logan tightened his grip on my hand. "You guys … knew?"

Cian scoffed. "It's not like either of you were that discrete. All of the staring and sighing, and it's not a secret that you're the only one she spends more than a few minutes with. We knew you were more than just her favorite."

I turned to Logan with an open mouth. This whole time I thought we were dancing on the outskirts, staying out of the way, and avoiding drawing any attention.

"And you're okay with it? With us?" he asked my siblings.

Cian brightened. "Of course. You're one of the best men I know. You've proven yourself time and time again. We know you care about our sister and will always take care of her. You've put her and her needs before your own for years, and I think I speak for all of us when I say that we're happy for you."

Aiden nodded. "I was expecting you to be the one to kidnap her and take her away when the suitors began arriving."

Charlie groaned and dropped her face in her hands.

Aiden looked confused. "What? Too soon?"

Serena threw her napkin at him. "Yes, Aiden. Much too soon."

He shrugged and returned his focus on me. "We're happy for you guys, that's the point."

"So you'll support us when we talk to Mum and Dad?" I asked hopefully.

Cian cringed, but Serena slapped his arm. He sighed. "Yes, we will."

"It would be helpful if we understood why they were so set on having the suitors come in the first place," Charlie pointed out. Aiden nodded.

Cian seemed to grow more uncomfortable, and I stared him down. "What do you know?"

He flinched and I knew he was hiding something.

"Cian, spill," Aiden barked at him.

"I'm not positive, okay? We were gone when Dad made the announcement, but I've heard him express some concerns recently that might have to do with this whole mess."

I waved my hands. "And? What are they?"

"He's worried about you and how you'll be taken care of. Things are a bit... muddy when it comes to your inheritance. Apparently, Duke McNally had something set aside for you, but it's gone."

"Who?" Logan cut in.

"My godfather," I answered. "He was my mother's uncle. He never had children of his own and my mum was quite close to him. His will stated that he left everything to me." I hadn't thought about this since he passed away last year. I was made aware of the inheritance, but I didn't know the details. I didn't need to. Mum had told me it was a large sum and it was up to me if I wanted to keep his properties. I told her to give those to other family members since I already had my cottage. The money was supposed to be in an account for when or if I ever needed it.

Cian looked uncomfortable. "Yes, well Mum's cousin has

come forward claiming that she found a more recent will in one of the properties and it says that everything should be divided amongst her family."

I shook my head. "Mum's sister and her children have been estranged from the rest of us for almost twenty years. No one would believe Uncle Ron would do that."

Cian shook his head. "It's under review. There are a team of attorneys working on it, but for now all of the assets are tied up and you don't have access to any of it."

I shrugged. "Okay. I was never planning on using it anyway."

"Yes, well, you may need to. Parliament is trying to pass a law to lower taxes, therefore reducing the Sovereign Grant. It also includes a stipulation that the heirs will stop receiving support after the age of twenty one."

"They're trying to stop us from getting money?" I needed to clarify.

"Yes. I won't be included in that, and neither will the next in line which is Aiden, until I have my own heir. So, when that time comes, you three will no longer be given payment."

I wasn't sure what to say without sounding like… well, a spoiled princess. "We sacrifice everything, our lives, our privacy, our safety for our country. How can they simply cut us off?"

Cian rubbed his jaw, looking more tired than I'd seen him in months, since Aiden stepped down from LochEnergy and took some responsibility off Cian's shoulders.

"Nothing's been passed yet, but Dad is worried about you and Rowan. Aiden still has shares of the company so he's set, but you two." He looked at me with pity, and I immediately recoiled.

"Cian, I'm a grown woman. I can get a job if I need to."

He signed. "No, you can't. That's the problem. You might have a degree from an excellent university and experience running charities, but no one will hire you. Can you imagine having the princess on your staff? No, they're putting you and Rowan in a position to lose."

"Who says I even need money? I have this house and my own investments and accounts that have been left to me."

"Plus, she has me. I'll provide for her," Logan added, and I squeezed his hand.

"I can't believe this is what has Dad so worried. I don't need or want millions a year."

"He just wants to make sure you continue to have the life you know," Aiden added. He seemed surprised by this news, but not as concerned as Cian was.

"Like Cian said, the bill hasn't been passed. The people might see it and laugh." Serena attempted a smile, which I appreciated.

"Thank you all for your concern, but I'll be fine. We'll be fine." I looked to Logan and smiled. I meant it when I said we could face anything together. One day later, and we were already tackling our first issue.

Charlie leaned forward and seemed to hesitate for a moment. "I don't know how to ask this without overstepping."

Cian laughed. "You're family. There is no overstepping."

She grinned. "It's just… the royal family, your parents, and you guys have other sources of income. Like Isla said, she has investments and property. It's not like if this bill becomes law, Isla and Rowan will be destitute and on the streets."

"You're right," Cian agreed. "Our family has been saving and making investments for generations. Our parents are worth quite a bit. They've been smart and kept things separate from the crown. That being said, I think Dad is acting out of concern for Isla. I think he wanted to make sure she married wealthy so she never had to worry. I don't agree with his choices, but I think he was coming from a place of love."

Knowing all of this did change my perspective. He thought he was taking care of me. He wasn't as perceptive as my siblings. I doubted he knew how Logan and I felt about each other. I hoped he didn't, at least.

"I think I need to have a talk with them."

"That's probably a good idea," Aiden teased.

"I'm glad you said that because… they're on their way," Cian said and jumped up, taking his plate to the sink then hurrying out of the room.

20

LOGAN

Never in all my time with the royal family had I seen any of them run away from a situation. As shocked as I was, it was nothing compared to Isla's expression.

"He called them?" she shrieked and turned to Aiden. "How could he do that to me?"

Aiden shrugged, clearly amused by it all. "It doesn't take a genius to figure out where you are, Isla. There's only one place you'd go."

She huffed and folded her arms. "I could have gone anywhere in the world."

He smiled gently like he was talking down a toddler from a tantrum. "You could have, yes. We all know you well enough to know there's only one place you go when you need to clear your head."

I smirked. She had made that exact point herself, but she wasn't impressed by her family's understanding of her personality.

"Fine. They can come, but that doesn't mean I need to talk to them. I came here for a reason. I wanted to be left alone. You guys coming was one thing, mum and dad is quite another."

She stood and politely excused herself from the room. I watched her head to the back porch and shook my head.

"Is it really a good idea for them to come here? I don't think she's ready to talk to them. I don't think she blames your parents for what happened, but she's still hurt by this dismissal of her opinion and feelings. She told them she didn't want men to come and they disregarded that. If the main concern really is money and her future, they should have told her. She's an adult, a smart one at that, and it's her life they're trying to control. She should have known all the facts and been allowed to make her own decision on how to move forward. If she chose then to entertain the idea of marrying a noble, then the invitation to the suitors should have been extended. Honestly, this was all so poorly handled. I can't help but agree with her refusal to speak to them."

I felt like I'd just poured out every thought and feeling I'd had about this onto Aiden, Charlie, and Serena. They had no more control over this than I did, but it felt good to vent. None of us could change the past and what happened. I knew there wasn't anything we could do, but I hoped everyone learned from this, and moving forward the family would be better about communicating.

"You're right, Logan. I don't agree with how my parents handled any of this. I agree there were many mistakes made. I'm on Isla's side. I know Cian is too. We'll support our sister, even against our parents. It's not only our duty as her brothers, but in this case, it's simply the right thing to do. We can face them together. If we present a united front, they will have to hear us out."

Charlie took her fiancé's hand and smiled. "I know it's too little too late, but hopefully we can learn from this."

Serena agreed. "I know what I won't be doing to my children."

It was a bit mind blowing to think about the fact that she was the future queen. This could very well be a situation she faced one day.

"Yes, please handle it better," Charlie said with a tease. "If I ever hear that you and Cian are forcing my poor niece or nephew into an arranged marriage I won't hesitate to stop you."

Aiden nodded. "Agreed."

Serena laughed. "I can promise you, that will never happen. You guys are forgetting one important piece of information." She leaned forward and met each of our gazes before continuing. "I'm American. We're all about personal freedoms and all that jazz."

Charlie giggled. "That's right. We're here to get everyone to lighten up and start new traditions."

Serena tilted her head and winked. "If anything, you and I will be getting in trouble for dismissing too many traditions."

I leaned back in my seat and smiled. There was a lot of change in our country's future, but I was grateful for it. Cian and Aiden found amazing, strong, independent women that would only encourage Lochland to make positive changes.

I hoped I would be seen in the same light. If things progressed to that. I shouldn't get too far ahead of myself, but that was where I wanted this to go. Building a future with Isla was more than I could ever want.

"So, Logan." Charlie put everyone's attention back on me. "How are you going to handle the king and queen?"

"I'm going to support Isla, of course."

Her grin turned wicked. "I mean, how are you going to ask for their blessing?"

I closed my eyes. After all this talk of Isla being an independent woman and moving the country forward, this felt like a giant leap backward. She wasn't a piece of property or item to be traded. I knew how important it was to gain the approval of her parents, but the matter had slipped my mind due to the chaos we'd been living in.

I sighed. "My biggest concern with admitting my feelings to Isla was not measuring up. Not being worthy of a woman like her. Not just because of her title, but who she is as a person. I believed she deserved more than me. I'm her guard, not a duke. I can't pretend like that doesn't still bother me, but it doesn't matter to her. She doesn't care about my station; she loves me and I love her. At the end of the day, our dedication to one another and our willingness to fight for one another is what matters."

Serena rested a hand on her chest. "That. Just say that and they will understand."

Charlie nodded. "That's beautiful."

"I meant every word."

Aiden leaned forward with his elbows on the table. "I'm sure you're nervous. You might see yourself as only her guard, but that's not what I see. You've honorably served and protected Lochland for six years. You've proven yourself to be brave, smart, trustworthy, and loyal. You're talented and a true leader. Cian and I have discussed it, and there's no one better for our sister. We trust you to care for her, and our parents will too."

Isla had said something similar to that before, but I assumed she was being too complimentary due to her romantic feelings for me. Hearing it from Aiden rocked me. I wasn't some lowly commoner in his eyes. Maybe it was only me who saw myself that way.

"Thank you, Aiden. That means more than I can say."

He nodded and stood, collecting the empty plates and glasses. Charlie helped him and they walked toward the sink together to begin cleaning. It was another sight I'd never thought I'd see, but it seemed I underestimated the princes.

Serena watched me and smiled when I met her eyes. "I know you're probably nervous. I was when I was in your position, but you have all of us supporting the two of you. Remember that."

With that, she stood and left the room.

It was time for me to find Isla and remind her she wasn't alone. Not anymore and never again.

Her parents arrived without their normal fanfare. I was sitting out back with Isla when Charlie peeked her head through the doorway and announced they were here and waiting for us in the front drawing room.

"Are you ready?" I asked Isla as I stood and took her hand.

She sighed and met my eyes. "Yeah, it's time for everything to be out in the open."

We walked through the hall and I paused at the stairs, out of hearing distance. "Do you want to talk to them alone first?"

She shook her head. "You and I are a team now. Anything they have to say to me is going to be shared with you so they're going to have to get used to it."

I admired her brazen attitude, but I wasn't sure the king and queen would be as pleased. Together we entered the room. Anne jumped up when she saw us and took Isla into her arms. Leo also stood and waited his turn to hug his daughter.

"Are you sure you're okay? Do you need a physician to come?" Anne held Isla's face between her palms and looked her over.

"I'm sure, Mum. I'm just fine." She looked to her dad for help. Leo placed his hand on his wife's arm, and they stepped back to sit down. We took the couch across from them. I felt the weight of their eyes on me.

"Logan, we appreciate all you've done for our family. We don't know how to ever properly express our gratitude," Anne gushed. I almost told her she could thank me by accepting me into their family, but that would probably be too much too soon.

"Of course, Your Majesty."

She waved me off. "You know better. Just Anne and Leo."

I nodded and waited for the king to speak. So far, he just stared at us.

Isla straightened her shoulders and addressed them. "I'm not sure where to start. There's been so much that's happened."

Leo lowered his chin. "Why don't you start with why you're here with Logan rather than at home?"

"I needed time to clear my head. I asked Logan to come because I felt safe with him and I wanted to spend time with him."

Anne looked between us, expressionless. Whatever she was thinking was a mystery to me.

Isla reached for my hand and gave it a squeeze. "I've had feelings for Logan for a while. He remained distant and professional, only allowing us to develop a friendship. When you announced that suitors would be invited to meet me, I tried to stop you because I knew my heart already belonged to him. I don't care about marrying a noble or some wealthy elitist. I want to be with Logan, and it took this experience to get him to accept and admit that he wants to be with me."

I smiled at her perspective of things. If only she knew the war that had raged inside me for months and months.

"You... you want to be with Logan?" Anne asked, sounding surprised.

Isla nodded. "I love him and he loves me."

Anne turned her attention to me. "Is that true?"

I nodded. "Yes, I love Isla very much. I've never let myself admit that to her because I didn't think I was worthy of her. I recognized I was too far below her station to be considered a suitable option. As her personal guard, I forced myself to remain professional and suppress any romantic feelings so I could continue to have a place in her life."

Leo remained silent which made my stomach tighten. I wanted him to say something, anything to let us know what he was thinking.

"So, you decided to settle for staying in her life as her guard rather than risk losing her completely?" Anne asked.

"Yes."

She sighed and clutched her chest. "Oh my. That's so romantic. You must love her very much."

I finally cracked a smile. "I do."

Isla turned to me and I met her gaze. She was right, we could face this together. If we survived this discussion, I knew we could overcome anything else life threw our way.

"I'm not sure what to say," Leo's voice filled the silence.

Anne patted his knee. "I'm very happy for both of you. I'm sure our recent actions might seem to contradict this, but we do want you to be happy. Everything we do is with that in mind."

Isla clenched my hand, and I held back a cringe. She needed me for strength, and I was going to give her that, no matter how much it ached.

"Then why didn't you guys tell me the truth? Why did you go through with bringing those men in when I asked you not to?"

The queen flinched, and Leo leaned forward. "We thought we were protecting you. There are things you don't know."

"So, tell me. You're trying to control my future, my life, without telling me everything."

Leo glanced at me and apparently decided he didn't mind my presence. "There's a bill."

Isla interrupted. "Yes, I know. It's trying to reduce taxes and limit what heirs get."

He sighed and nodded. "I didn't want to worry you. I was trying to make sure you would always be provided for."

"I'm an adult, Dad. You should have just told me what was going on and we could have had a discussion about what to do next. Inviting strangers into our home to arrange a loveless marriage was wrong. You hurt me deeply by keeping things from me."

"We never meant to hurt you, darling." Anne's voice was full of remorse.

"This just proves you don't trust me or respect me as an individual."

"That's not what our intent was. We were trying to protect you," Leo seemed to plead with Isla.

"I understand your intentions. I do, but I asked you not to go through with it."

I feared this was going to go in circles and we were here to accomplish something. "We hope to move forward. Isla and I love each other and want to start a life together. I might not have a title or wealth like the other men, but I know I can make your daughter happy. I know we can get through challenges together and overcome anything thrown our way. I might not be able to provide her with a lavish lifestyle. I don't offer much to the crown in the way of alliances. I don't own a company that can create jobs and boost the economy in Lochland, but I can give her love and support. I can make her happy and keep her safe and protected. I'm humbled she feels the same way about me. We're going to be together, but it would mean a great deal to us to know we have your blessing."

Leo stared me down for several intimidating moments before he stood. "I think this is a conversation we should have alone."

I squeezed Isla's hand once before getting up and following my king out of the room. I kept my expression blank but my insides were knotted and pushing their way up my throat.

21

ISLA

I didn't get a chance to ask Logan what my father said to him. Once they were done, Dad spoke quietly with Mum, then insisted we all return to the palace. Cian and Aiden didn't even protest. So much for having my back and facing our parents together. Logan avoided me while we loaded into the helicopter, and the moment we landed in Ballivaughn he disappeared.

"What's going on?" I grabbed Aiden's shoulder and made him turn to face me.

He seemed uncomfortable, but I was sick of the whispers and texts. Even though everyone tried to be discrete I caught them texting when they thought I wasn't watching on our trip home.

"I'm not entirely sure. Logan told me and Charlie that you guys were ready to come home so we got your things packed and met out front."

"He didn't tell you what Dad said to him?" This was getting strange. Why was Logan running away?

"No, he didn't."

I nodded and headed through the back entrance of the

palace toward the stairs. I was ready for a nice long bath. If Logan was going to avoid me, then I could give him the space to do it. On the flight to the palace, my mind went through every possibility of what could have happened when Logan left the room with my father, but it was making me crazy. Had it gone well? Did Dad give his blessing? Did he say no? What if he threatened to have him reassigned on the other side of the country or deployed halfway around the world?

There were too many options and not all of them were good. I wasn't going to chase him down and force him to talk before he was ready. If he needed space, then I could give him that. Afterall, he'd done the same for me.

I stepped into my room and stared at my bed. I waited for a flashback or memory of the night I was taken, but nothing came. It was a small mercy. There was no dread or fear of being in here. It was still my space, my sanctuary. That hadn't been taken from me. I moved through to the bathroom and started the water to fill the tub. A long soak was just what I needed.

My mind wandered again as I undressed and stepped into the warmth. I sank in, rested my head back, and closed my eyes. Maybe Dad gave him an assignment. Or told him he had to do something before we'd receive their blessing.

I tried to stop thinking and just relax, but that only lasted a few minutes. A knock came from the suite door, but I ignored it. I was taking some necessary me-time. Everything else could wait.

"Princess?"

I groaned and dipped further into the water. Carolyn would wait until I replied, no matter how long I took.

"Yes?"

"I know you just got back, but your attendance is required at an event tonight. You need to be ready by five."

When I got in the bath it was close to three so I knew I needed to hurry. "What event?"

"One of the hospitals," she replied.

I didn't remember seeing a hospital event on the calendar this week, but since my schedule had been commandeered by my father I might have missed the notice.

"I'll be ready."

"Let me know if you need me."

I listened for the sound of her walking away before I slammed my fist into the water. I just wanted a moment of peace. Was it asking too much for just a few days for myself?

Of course, I wanted to support the hospital and be there for the unveiling of a children's wing. I was passionate about the work and I loved seeing the kids, but not today.

This was why I wanted to stay at my cottage. I needed time off the grid, well at least the palace's grid. I needed time to decompress and make sure I was back at my best so I could be completely present when it mattered. Now I was going to be forced to smile and pretend for the evening while my mind was focused on what was going on with Logan. Hopefully Cian and Serena would be there as well. I could use them as a distraction so no one realized how scattered I was.

Finally admitting I was pushing it, I left the safety of the bath and went through the motions of getting ready relying on muscle memory while doing my hair and makeup. I slipped on a pale green shift dress and cream heels before walking out to my sitting area where Carolyn waited. She looked up from her folder and smiled.

"I'm so happy to see you back, safe and happy."

I tried to smile but it fell flat. I wasn't necessarily happy. Yes, I was glad to be home and not locked away in a strange place, but my confusion with Logan was overshadowing that.

"Are Cian and Serena attending as well?"

She nodded briefly. "Yes, but they've already left. Cian needed to arrive early to sign a few things."

She stood and we walked out to the hall. Shane smiled at me when he saw me. "Welcome home, Isla."

"Thank you, Shane. And thank you again for being there. For coming for me."

He seemed uncomfortable by my words but he nodded. "Of course."

I continued down to the main stairs and I noticed Carolyn had fallen behind. I stopped and looked over my shoulder. "Is something wrong?"

She looked up from her phone and shook her head. "No, sorry. Just letting one of the committees know that we're moving the meeting to next week."

I waited for her to finish before continuing down. "Is everything ready for Independence Day?"

"Yes, everything has been booked and scheduled. I'm starting my confirmation calls next week so nothing will wait until the last minute."

"Thanks so much for staying on top of everything. These past few weeks have been rough, but you've been so amazing for picking up my slack."

She smiled and ducked her head. "It's my job, Isla. You know I'm always here for you."

"I do." I almost hugged her but stopped. She wasn't a fan of affection, and I knew better than to push her.

"Welcome back, Princess." A butler I vaguely recognized bowed as he opened the door for me.

"Thank you." I took the steps but paused when I realized there wasn't a car waiting. "Carolyn?"

I turned to ask here where it was, but I realized she wasn't behind me. The doors were shut and I was alone. I looked around, suddenly feeling like something was wrong. Had I walked into a trap? But Carolyn wouldn't set me up.

"Isla."

I spun at the sound of my name and smiled when I spotted Logan walking along the path that led around the palace.

"Logan, are you done avoiding me?" I looked around again. "I'm not sure how much time I have to chat. I'm supposed to be heading to a hospital."

He smiled and stopped a few feet from me. He was wearing a simple charcoal sweater and grey pants. Much more casual than I was used to seeing him. If he wasn't in uniform then he was in a suit. Even at the cottage he stayed in a black shirt and black tactical pants. This outfit was more along the lines of what Cian and Aiden wore when they weren't in public.

"I'm sorry about earlier. There were some things I needed to sort through. Then as soon as we got here, I needed to take care of something that was fairly time sensitive."

"I understand." I only partially did. It still felt like he was keeping something from me. "Were you able to get everything done?"

He nodded. "Yes, it's all sorted."

"Good." Where was the car? Surely, I was going to be late.

"Isla, will you take a walk with me?"

"I'm not sure I can, Logan. I've an event to go to."

He reached for my hand and led us down the path he'd come from. "There's no event. Don't worry."

"What? Then why did Carolyn say…" I trailed off when the realization that he must have been responsible for that sank in. "What are you up to?"

He gave me a heart melting smile but said nothing.

We passed the garden and continued out to the edge of the lake, close to where we'd practiced archery just days before. That felt like another lifetime.

Finally, he stopped and faced me. "Isla, there's something

I need to tell you. I want you to know that I did it because I wanted to. This is truly my own choice."

I narrowed my eyes and waited for him to spill whatever he was keeping from me.

He sighed. "I'm no longer an active duty Marine. My sergeant accepted my resignation and as of today I'm a normal citizen."

I gasped. This was an option he mentioned, but I expected him to think about it for a while, really consider what it would mean. "Really?"

He nodded. "Yes, and also as of today I'm head of security for the palace."

I let out a laugh. "What? What does that mean?"

"There are some changes and improvements that need to be made around the palace, and I'll be leading those efforts. I'll no longer be a guard, but I will advise on their training."

"So, you're working in the palace?"

He nodded. "Your father offered me the position this morning."

I shook my head. "This was what he pulled you away to talk about?"

His smile grew. "This and one other thing."

"Oh yeah? What's that?"

He held my gaze for a few seconds before getting down on his knee. I gasped and covered my mouth with my free hand.

"He said that he and your mum support us and want us to be happy. He told me to not waste a moment and never let you forget how much I love you. So, Isla I want you to know that I love you more and more with each day. I know we have a long road ahead of us, but I want to face it all with you. I want to learn everything about you. I want all of you, forever. Will you make me the happiest man in the world and agree to marry me?"

"Yes, Logan. Of course." He slipped the most beautiful emerald and diamond ring onto my finger and I burst into tears. It was my grandmother's wedding ring. I'd admired it for years but never imagined Mum would let me have it. I thought the cottage would be all I'd have of my grandparents, but now I had a daily reminder of them and their love.

He stood and I pulled him toward me, pressing my lips to his. This was the very first moment of the rest of our lives. I wanted to remember every single detail, but all that mattered was how I felt. I was going to be happy. I knew that to my bones. No matter what happened with the bill or my inheritance or Logan's job, we would be happy.

I broke the kiss and beamed up at him. "I didn't expect this."

He matched my smile. "Me either, but after your father spoke to me, things moved quickly. When we got back, your mum took me to the safe and gave me the ring. I didn't tell either of them I wanted to propose, but they seemed to know. I debated waiting but I couldn't. I want to be with you forever and didn't want to wait a second longer."

"Me either. We can have a nice long engagement if you want."

He shook his head. "We'll get married as soon as the madness around your brothers' weddings settles down.

He'd already thought about it? That was enough to make me kiss him again. "I love you, Logan. Thank you for taking a chance on me."

He ran his thumb along my cheek. "I'm the luckiest man in the world."

Thanks for reading! I hope you enjoyed Isla and Logan's story!
Word of mouth is so important for authors to succeed. If you enjoyed Her Royal Rebellion, I'd love for you to leave a review on Amazon!

Keep Reading,
Xoxo B

Brittney has been an avid reader for as long as she can remember. Her parents' form of punishment growing up was taking away her books and making her go outside to play. She loves the beach, exercising, sleeping in, and cookies. Yes, she does know those contradict each other. She's an obsessive dog lover and is slowly learning to appreciate the mountains she lives in. Nature can be okay, sometimes.

> Find out more about Brittney and her books at
> www.Brittneymulliner.com

Made in the USA
Columbia, SC
18 July 2022